Vanessa Palmer's
CHOOSE YOUR OWN ROMANTIC ADVENTURE

Choose Your Own Romantic Adventure
Copyright © 2018 by Vanessa Palmer

All rights reserved. No part of this publication may be reproduced, distributed, or transmitted in any form or by any means, including photocopying, recording, or other electronic or mechanical methods, without the prior written permission of the author, except in the case of brief quotations embodied in critical reviews and certain other non-commercial uses permitted by copyright law.

Tellwell Talent
www.tellwell.ca

ISBN
978-1-77370-745-7 (Paperback)

Acknowledgments and Dedication

I would like to thank my mom and dad, of course. Thank you, Mumma, for giving me emotional support and encouraging my love of writing. I don't know if you will ever understand how much it has meant to me to have someone always there to read my stories, and praise them, no matter how small or odd. And thank you, Dad, for giving me sound advice and for paying for half of this book so it could be made. I know this is not exactly what you want me to put all my effort into, and it means spending a lot of your money, but I would not have survived without the safety and security you've gifted me with. I love you both. I should also thank my sister—but she's not old enough to read this book. So, to my sister in the future, if she ever goes back and reads this, hopefully now you understand why I would not let you read my first book all those years ago.

I would also like to thank Mark Fischbach, also known as Markiplier. In truth, I have not met Mark in real life, but I feel I still need to thank him for being there for me. There were many a times when I felt so alone and worthless, and, on occasion, had some *very* dark thoughts; and even though my family has always been there for me, sometimes it was Mark that would help me most. He will probably never see this, but, thank you, Mark, for telling me I can do anything, for telling me you care and, most importantly, for always being there when I need cheering up.

Finally, I would like to dedicate this book to my self-esteem. I know you are tiny and fragile, and I hope that when you are hurting you will look back on this book and grow strong from it.

How To Read This Book

Don't worry, it's not complicated.

First, read the opening part, which can be found on the next page. At the end of the part you will find two possible actions you can take, each with a corresponding page number. Choose one of the options and flip to the page number corresponding to that option.

Continue doing this until you come to The End. At this point you have finished that path, but it's not over! Now you are free to start again and try another route.

Don't forget to mark your ending in the completion list at the back of the book!

Where It All Starts

You sit on a bar stool glancing around the room, surveying all the celebrities of high society. You've only ever seen them in the media, if at all, and you're feeling a tad out of place. You may have put on your best outfit, but it can't compare to the masterpieces the other women are wearing; their colourful—and sometimes odd—gowns swim between the simple black suits that comprise the vast majority of the men's attire.

The sound of clicking high heels and low mumble of small talk just barely overpowers the band huddled together in the closed-off corner beside the dance floor. The smell of alcohol and generously-applied perfume and colognes had assaulted you the moment you walked in, but over the hour you've been here it has started to become more tolerable.

It was a lot to take in at first and, having already tried adventuring out into the crowd beforehand, it still feels like you could get lost amongst these people. You know some of them, but they know nothing of you, and mentioning that the only reason you were here was "because of your friend" hadn't really left the best impression. Maybe they assumed you were some sort of hyperactive fangirl who had shown up to gawk at the celebrities—or were there to gain something, like the people you occasionally heard making business propositions, or the people offering to be someone's partner for the night. Either way, by now you've pretty much given up on any attempt to speak to these people who seem like they're from a totally different world.

Luckily, the elderly yet kind-faced bartender shows you sympathy, having noticed how awkward and out-of-place you're acting in the regal atmosphere. He couldn't give you free drinks, but he has been continuously refilling your glass of water between his many other customers, and letting you sit there in peace.

Occasionally, people walk up to the bar and order a drink, possibly sparing you a quick smile or greeting while they wait before disappearing back into the sea of sparkling gowns and suits. If they happen to take one of the bar stools, it's several seats down from your own, which gives them space to chat with whoever followed them over.

The whole party, though a spectacle to look at, leaves an emptiness inside and around you. It's as if the other attendees can sense how out of place you are and are subconsciously backing away, leaving you to blankly stare out into the crowd or at the glass of water you're holding.

Finally, your staring eyes and blank mind come into focus when three card-sized pieces of paper are smacked down—rather roughly—in front of you, like a frustrated poker player folding his hand.

"Every time," says a woman in a hushed voice, teetering on the edge of an exclamation.

You look up and over your shoulder to find your friend, who is also the reason you're here at this unexpectedly boring party.

"Just because I'm single doesn't mean I want every geez— ... *elderly* man asking me for a 'private night' together." She corrects herself, apparently having difficulty keeping her sweetheart celebrity act up. She takes a seat beside you and slips off her three-inch heals for a couple blissful minutes. You turn each slip of paper over and towards you so you can see all the phone numbers laid out; one even has "300$/night" written on it.

"Creeps," she mumbles under her breath, but she glances around anyways to make sure you were the only one who heard, feeling paranoid of not knowing when and where the paparazzi could be.

She proceeds to order a drink and chat at you for a bit. She politely complains about how she had to be nice to everyone as she's new to the industry, but you listen, as it fills a bit of the empty night. You don't complain until she brings up how reclusive you're being.

"And what's with you hiding over here at the bar? I didn't drag you hear so you could be a wallflower," she scolds in a light tone.

She may be frustrated but she's not truly mad at you. Maybe she even feels a little sympathy seeing as she herself has had a challenging time dealing with the veterans who saw her as "nouveau riche."

"Or are you too distraught about Andrew not showing up that you can't bear to look at anyone else?" she says semi-dramatically, poking fun at how the possibility of meeting Andrew Smyth was the deciding factor on whether you would attend tonight.

Mr. Andrew Smyth is an actor (and one-time cookbook writer, oddly enough). You've recently discovered him and, having taken a liking to the six-foot-three, toned man, have a bit of a celebrity crush on him—or so your friend has decided in her own mind. You'd looked up his filmography, created a to-watch list as you read up on his previous films, and watched as many interviews as YouTube provided. He was kind and gentlemanly—"because I'm Canadian," he had joked in several interviews. He was passionate about both his roles and charity work. He was attractive, with ink black hair and seemingly unnaturally-bright forest green eyes; he was intelligent, he was talented, and your friend warned you that it might all be a show.

Everyone looks and acts better when on camera, but they may be different in a more casual setting. She even went so far as to point out the well-supported rumour that he was a womanizer.

"He may not show up with girls on his arms," she had warned you, "but, supposedly, he always leaves with one, or more."

That and the fact that he was supposedly developing a drinking problem.

These things clashed with your romanticized version of Andrew; so, despite understanding that, in reality, he was different than how you imagined him, you tended to ignore the rumours. It was just a celebrity crush, a fantasy you sometimes indulged in.

"Try looking for someone you actually like rather than a fantasy you're putting over a real guy," your friend suggests, noticing your focus had shifted from the conversation.

You look back over at her and, just as you began to reply, someone—obviously unintentionally—interrupts you. You don't recognize them, but your friend gives you a look that suggests she does, and you should too.

Once noticing you the person apologizes, asking if they were interrupting. Your friend waves off their concern and flashes you with pleading eyes. Whoever this was, it is important to your friend that she speak with them, so you assure them that they weren't interrupting and let them whisk her away to chat, leaving you alone once again.

You sit there, considering if you should simply leave, when a smooth voice clutches your attention.

"Is this seat taken?" he asks. Out of the corner of your eye you see a man gesture towards the seat to your right. It seems like an innocent enough question, until you consider the fact that at least three seats on either side of you are empty, but he's asking to sit right beside you.

Will you let him sit with you? This may be your chance to switch your lonely night into something a little more entertaining than staring at the rich and the famous.

Then again, it might be one of those men your friend had to deal with, some older man looking for a girl to take home. Maybe it's best to just cut your losses and head home.

Let Him Sit With You ➲ PAGE 129
Get Up And Go Home ➲ PAGE 78

ABANDON ATTEMPT TO TALK

You pull Andrew's hand closer, leading his fingers so they cup you. Though it's obvious your attempt at conversation had thrown him off, you both silently agree to return to the original plan.

Andrew's movements are stilted. He pauses occasionally to look into your eyes, as if expecting you to shove him away any minute. And sometimes you do, as his fast pace and random pauses to look at you sceptically are making some moments awkward, and, at times, uncomfortable. It doesn't help that even though your bodies are pressed together—shallow breaths mixing in between slow kisses—Andrew seems so very distant. He may be with you physically, but mentally he is so far away.

Even when your foreplay has to be put on hold so you can transfer from the limo to his house, he doesn't seem at all interested in you as a person. He doesn't speak a word, barely even looking at you as he leads you into his home.

He unlocks one of two doors acting as the front entrance and slips in before holding the door open for you to follow. You enter into a short hallway that leads to a massive living room. The hallway is empty except for a door to your left and a desk against the right wall with a landline phone sitting atop it.

You're about to pass said phone when it springs to life, making Andrew jerk back slightly. Its ring is rather loud and comes from a couple places deeper in the house as well as the phone beside you.

Andrew picks up the receiver but doesn't answer it quite yet.

"Could you wait for me in there?" He points to the door opposite the desk.

You oblige, entering the room where you find a conveniently placed bedroom that even comes with a small bathroom. A guest bedroom, if you were to guess by how clean it was, and without a touch of personal items anywhere.

As you prepare yourself for the inevitable, you can hear snippets of Andrew's phone conversation from just outside the door.

"Really? ... No, that's great ... Look, can we talk about this tomorrow? I kind of have company right now ... Can we not start this again? ... I'm just—... Maybe one day—... Alright ... Have a good night ... Bye."

You hear the click of the phone being placed back into its base, and Andrew enters the room not long after.

"Sorry about that," is all he seems willing to say about it. Considering how your last attempt at conversation went—not to mention people's right to privacy—you don't pry any further.

He disrobes on his own, grabs a couple necessary items from a rather stocked drawer beside the bed, and takes charge. His continued distance creates an awkward feeling of disinterest; it's apparent he knows how to please a lady, but the feeling of pleasure is weakened by shimmers of something like regret that occasionally slip through.

After the deed is done, breath still heavy from his climax, Andrew slips out of the bed, gathers his clothing, and—without a word or even a shared look—leaves on slightly wobbly legs.

Is this his signal for you to leave? You two have accomplished what you came here for, is there anything left for you to stay for? A chance to make amends to the rocky start of a possible relationship?

Or perhaps you're simply too tired to drag yourself out of the bed right now. He hasn't specifically told you to leave right at this moment, and the bed is so warm compared to the chill of the room. A night's sleep might be welcome.

Fall Asleep ◆ PAGE 75
Leave Right After Sex ◆ PAGE 119

ACCEPT IT

You accept the cab ride—it's probably all you're going to get from Andrew.

"Wonderful. Please, come with me." Andrew puts on a charming smile and walks you out of the room.

Using the phone sitting atop a desk by the front door, he calls up a cab company.

"Hey, it's Andrew … Yes … Thank you … See you soon." Is all he needs to say, proving even more how common this is for him.

He is kind enough to wait with you at the door until your ride arrives, but the conversation is difficult. He's polite and calm, but the circumstances make any kind words from him seem false.

"Have a good day," Andrew calls as you get into the cab, waving goodbye to you like you're a client leaving a restaurant.

The End

AGREE TO LEAVE

Although Andrew's inability to ask you to leave himself is rude, you accept this is how it's ending. It had been clear from the beginning that Andrew's interest in you was a fleeting physical attraction, so him treating this as a one-night stand is not surprising. If anything, at least he was kind enough to have your clothes washed and offer you a shower.

The man strips the bed of its sheets and places them in a wheel-adorned opal red hamper. He allows you to take your leave without supervision. As you prepare to go, you consider what just transpired: the chance meeting, the steamy night, and how open and shut the case was.

What would have happened if you had chosen to do something different? Would it have even made a difference?

The End

ASK FOR SEX INSTEAD

When you bring up the idea, Andrew is so taken aback that he just stares at you for some time. His mouth opens and closes pointlessly like a fish, his cheeks reddening to the shade of a Koromo koi's scales.

"I didn't think you were interested, to be honest. Not that it bothers me, quite the opposite really."

He strolls towards you, smile showing something quite different than what it had mere seconds ago. "I just hope I haven't bored you with all my talking."

Andrew regains his composure, becoming an experienced-yet-cordial man. His arm slides around your waist and gently guides the two of you together. Even with so little space separating you, Andrew desires to be closer. He leans down and captures your lips, giving just one slow kiss before resting his forehead against yours. His eyes open to show a twinkle in them.

"Let's head upstairs."

As you follow Andrew's lead, you can make out a rush of opal red and some furniture in the large living room just past the small entrance hall. But you don't get much of a look otherwise as you're all too focused on Andrew who is gently holding your hand and leading you up a staircase. You go up to a second floor comprised of mostly an indoor balcony looking over the living room. You slip into the first door and gaze around a dimly lit bedroom.

"How bright would you like the lights?" He asks you. It's the first of many questions, all based around your preferences; they swoop in smoothly, like a bird flying over water yet not disturbing the flow: "Is this OK? Where would you like me? How does this feel?"

Along with the questions come feather-light touches that make your heart pump faster.

It ends the same as your next day begins—with Andrew smiling down at you like he couldn't believe his luck.

"Good afternoon," Andrew greets you, his fingers running through your hair, tempting you to drift back unconsciousness. "How did you sleep?"

He lays besides you and listens, simply enjoying this calm moment to watch you and take in your voice.

Once you answer, he asks yet another question. "How do you feel? Not sore anywhere, I hope."

Thankfully, you're not in any pain, though you can feel the remnants of last night, which is, sadly, a little uncomfortable now.

Andrew's hand leaves your hair and slides down your side until it reaches your thigh. "Would you like a shower?" It's clear from the way he massages your thigh that the shower he's offering would not be a lonely one. "And perhaps after, if you aren't busy, you could spend the day here."

A day-long date after the night you just had? It seems as if Andrew might be looking for something a little longer than a one-night stand. At least that was what he was conveying with how hope played in his eyes.

Then again, aren't there a few things you were planning to do today? You weren't expecting to be where you are this morning. If you start hanging out with Andrew now, who knows how long you could stay, and, unfortunately, there are responsibilities in life that should be taken care of.

Shower With Him ❯ PAGE 149
Ask To Go Home ❯ PAGE 18

ASK TO GO HOME

When you ask, Andrew falls silent. His eyes look to you, silently asking something before he turns.

"Sure, if that's what you want," he says. His voice hitches and his hurt tone leaks out for just a moment. His expression is pretty much blank, and he keeps his emotions under lock, not speaking again for quite some time. The two of you get dressed and he walks you to the door, but he stays silent and won't look you in the eye. He seems mentally far off, as if he's trying to decode something in his head.

It's not until you walk out the front door of his home that he finally speaks up.

"Hey."

Andrew grabs hold of the end of your outfit, holding it carefully between two fingers like a nervous child. "Did I do something wrong, maybe upset you in some way?" He begins to roll the fabric between his fingers and his eye contact drifts away. "I just thought things were going really well, you know?"

Were they? Is he, perhaps, mistaken? Maybe you want to explain that you simply have some responsibilities you need to attend to.

Or perhaps he is right in one way. Maybe you are worried about not what he has done wrong, but what he could do wrong in the future. He has such a bad reputation from too many reliable sources to make his sincerity seem like anything more than you being his pet of the week. Ending it now may save you from more hurt later on.

Leave Without Answering ➡ PAGE 123
Reassure Him ➡ PAGE 24

ASK TO SEE HIM

When you ask, the man looks at you quietly for a long moment, his judging eyes eventually melting into a look of annoyed sympathy.

"He ain't gonna care, but sure. Just wait here okay?" He does not wait for your answer before leaving.

You take a seat on the half-stripped bed and wait. It is a boring quarter hour but eventually Andrew appears, his smile forced and tired compared to his cocky grin last night.

"Good morning," he says, choosing to stay in the doorway rather than approaching you. He has changed into new clothing, a simple baggy shirt and sweat pants. "Is there something you wanted to say? I assume that's why you called me down here." Andrew leans sideways for a moment as he lets the man who woke you up pass by. "If not, I wouldn't mind calling you a cab."

Again with his verbally pushes towards the door. Perhaps this is just how Andrew does things, not just the man who has returned to striping the bed. With this second confirmation that you are expected to leave, maybe it's best to give up.

Or, are you unsatisfied with this abrupt ending? You were having a wonderful time with him at the party, chatting and dancing together. Could you just throw that away because you've finished having sex?

Accept It ➔ PAGE 14
Say You Want More ➔ PAGE 146

ASK TO SEE HIS PROJECT

Andrew stops in his tracks, his flirty smile drifting into a look that asks you to repeat yourself, as if he's not sure he heard you correctly. You explain your interest in his work, in him personally, and, although he keeps an air of confusion, he looks to the floor, his cheeks receiving a thin veil of pink.

"I would be happy to show you, if you really are interested." He turns to walk away but offers you his hand. "This way."

You take it, his grip as strong as a shy teenager on his first date.

He leads you through a rather opal red living room before descending some stairs into a dining room. The walls, the shelves—they're all packed full of family memorabilia, along with some important-looking papers. But you don't get the chance to gaze into these windows to Andrew's past as he is quick to pull out a stack of papers, decorating swatches and a laptop.

"It's a good thing you're here, I've been having some trouble deciding things. How hungry are you?"

This was the first of many questions. After asking if you had heard of the cookbook he had written, he explains that he's in the process of building his very own restaurant. He'll play the role of an owner, deciding how the restaurant looks and what they would serve, but he won't work in it, so he can still act.

But rather than explaining, Andrew mostly asks for your opinion. He's having trouble deciding on what the interior will look like and what to put on the menu. He could have simply given you a list of dishes he was interested in, but instead he begins cooking. He offers you different foods, asking which ones go well together, which seem unique, and what he could tweak in each recipe.

The more he speaks, the more passionate he becomes. Even when you admit to not loving a dish, he gains an intense vigour in fixing it. For once tonight, he doesn't look like he's trying to act suave. He's far too focused on his food, running in and out of the kitchen, waistcoat becoming dirtier with each trip. He doesn't slow down until you show interest in stopping.

"I'm sorry, are you tired?" he apologizes after a yawn forces its way out of you.

"What time is it?" he asks himself, leaning down to check his laptop. "Six in the morning! My goodness." He stands straight again. "I didn't mean to keep you up so late, let me show you to a bedroom."

Andrew practically pulls you from your seat and ushers you up the stairs. Not just to the main floor but up onto a second floor, this one consisting of an indoor balcony looking over the opal red living room and three doors. Despite how hasty his shift was from asking you questions to putting you to bed, Andrew is sure to go slow; he stops whenever you feel the need to, and holds you steady when your tired body starts to waver. You enter the middle room and, for a moment, it looks as if he intends to tuck you into bed as well, but he stops himself in the doorway.

"I'll leave you here then?" he says, starting to back away suddenly, as if frightened by what he would do if he stayed. It takes him a while to actually turn away from you. His eyes stare at yours and he smiles like a man putting his wife to bed. "Sweet dreams."

Thankful, you close the blinds to the room before sliding into bed, which allows you to get a full night—or day—of sleep, despite the sun coming up.

You don't wake until the afternoon, when the sun is already beginning to set. You take your slow, sweet time getting out of bed and prepare yourself before emerging from the bedroom. When you do, however, a sense of alienation washes over you: you're standing in an unfamiliar home with no one to guide you.

You wander downstairs, uncertain on what to do, and start looking around.

The room looks large and uncommonly tall, what with there not being a full second floor. The back wall is made of glass—a large window looking out into the setting sun illuminating the opal red furniture. Everything looks pristine, as if it had been ripped out of a magazine; pretty but devoid of any personal touches such as pictures. Those were all downstairs, you suppose. There is, however, one decoration that looks rather out of place.

There's a cheap-looking stand on a shelf against the wall, opposite the staircase, showing off three colourful circles.

You wander closer, realizing they're coins. There's no labelling on the clear, plastic casing to indicate what they are, but etchings in the coins themselves give away their use. One side has a triangle with words written around and on it with a number inside. *To Thine Own Self Be True* is scribed around the edge of the coin, and the words *Unity*, *Service*, and *Recovery* are along each edge of the triangle. Each thing in the triangle is different, however: One states *24 Hours*, one has *1 Month* and the last a decoration of *2 Months*. They are all to celebrate how long someone has been sober from alcohol—they are Alcoholics Anonymous coins.

You take time to soak in this information, after which you are left to decide what to do. Now, however, you have a slight scratching feeling at the back of your mind that you have intruded on something private of Andrew's, even if it is on display in his living room.

Should you leave now when no one is around to see you? Did this revelation about Andrew cause you to become uncomfortable? Or perhaps you simply want to go home, feeling that there's nothing else keeping you here.

Or does the thought of leaving or, more specifically, the thought of how Andrew would feel when he finds out you left, drive you to stay? It's not like you have to wait around, you could go search for him. You've been to all the floors, so it wouldn't take that long to find him.

Go Looking For Him ➡ **PAGE 88**
Don't Look For Him ➡ **PAGE 64**

REASSURE HIM

Somehow Andrew had gotten the wrong impression. And now that you know this, you assure him you wanting to leave was not because of him, it was the responsibilities of life that are pulling you away for the time being.

"Really? Good," Andrew says, looking only a bit relieved, like the harder question was yet to come. "… if that's the case," he added as a mumble to himself.

He backs off from the doorway but doesn't go far. He stops beside the long desk and leans over, grabbing a pen and scribbling something down on the notepad. He completes his note, rips it from the notepad and returns to you.

"Would you be willing to …" Andrew holds out the note paper he had just written on, his hand is shaking slightly and he has a nervous but hopeful smile, one you would expect a middle-schooler to have when asking their first crush on a date, "… call me later?"

The End

CALL AN AMBULANCE

Better safe than sorry. You pull out your phone and dial 911. A calm but stern-sounding woman answers the phone and takes in your situation. As you relay information, Andrew begins to lean more of his weight on you and his legs begin to wobble. Blood begins sliding down his chin and neck, soaking into his undershirt and waistcoat. His eyes start blinking faster before finally sliding shut.

It feels like an eternity until help arrives, but what a weight is lifted off your shoulders when the ambulance sirens pierce the quiet night! When Andrew hears them, however, he flinches back, curling further into you like he's disturbed in his sleep. Nor does he seem pleased when two paramedics start touching and moving him.

"Wait, wait," Andrew mumbles, eyes wandering dizzily as he stretches out a hand and starts grabbing at things.

"Sir, you need to stay still!" the male paramedic orders as he tries to strap Andrew down to the gurney and transfer him into the ambulance.

"No, wait." Andrew starts to shift and wriggle, his hand stretches further out in your direction. Then, your name passes his increasingly panicked and tired lips.

"Is that you?" The female paramedic's head whips around to face you, expression so serious it looks as if she's angry with you.

"Any chance you can keep him still? We need to check for glass shards in his head, but we can't do that if he's moving around."

It was most definitely an order rather than a suggestion, and one that you comply with.

You grab hold of Andrew's reaching hand and inform him that you're there with him. He settles instantly, squeezing your hand with the slightest of grip, and lets out a sigh of relief.

With this stillness you're able to transfer into the ambulance; you're being allowed to come along with them. You sit there as the paramedics survey Andrew's head, pulling back his hair to reveal large cuts in his scalp. Shards of glass shine through rivers of blood, making it a bit easier for the paramedics to pull out the larger shards.

As the paramedics work, you're occasionally forced to release his hand. Each time Andrew's arm stretches out for you and little whines escape his tired throat until you make contact with him again.

Finally, you make it to the hospital and follow behind the doctors for as long as you can, loosely holding on to Andrew's practically limp hand until you're stopped. You don't even have time to give Andrew any words of encouragement before he is whisked away behind a pair of swinging doors, a nurse holds out her arm in front of it like a barrier stopping cars while a train goes by.

"Sorry, Miss, but the police would like to speak to you." The nurse points down the hall at two policemen who notice you looking and start to approach you.

Though a bit hostile at first, they become more sympathetic as you honestly answer their questions about what happened. They even share an "Ahh" in realization when you describe the man that had attacked Andrew.

"He just got released for probation," one says, assuring you that they will find him quickly.

Once they've gathered enough information, they lead you to the desk where you're asked to give any piece of information you have on the patient. They ask for name, address, phone number, allergies, but all you can answer is what you know from interviews and media, which aren't always correct. The man behind the desk accepts your lack of personal knowledge on the patient, decides to call a family member they have on Andrew's file, and releases you. By the time you get to the waiting room it's roughly five in the morning. You sit and wait until a bit past six.

At that point, a woman, about 50 years of age, comes running down the hall. Her eyes are bloodshot and her outfit is something clearly thrown on last minute. Two younger women chase behind her, they look like they're a bit more in control of their emotions.

"Andrew, is he OK?" the woman yells, tears already streaking down her makeup-free face.

"Mom, calm down," says the older of the two girls, trying to place a soothing hand atop her mother's arm. The older woman pushes it away in exchange for a hug.

"I'm so scared, I was supposed to be the first to go," the older woman sobs. She doesn't seem to care about the people around looking on with either concern or annoyance.

"I am so sorry, Miss, but the doctors are still working with him. You'll have to wait here with his friend." The nurse raises a hand in your direction and the family members turn to you. Before anyone can say a word, the double doors swing open and a doctor walks out, then steps aside to let a gurney roll out of the room.

"Andrew!" the mother screams, practically throwing herself atop her kin.

"Please, ma'am, let us transfer him to his room first," the doctor who had opened the door says, placing his hand on the front of her shoulder and pushing her a safe distance away from Andrew.

"Is he alright? What happened?" The woman runs through a series of questions while the doctor attempts to answer as fast as she shoots them off.

"He will be fine," is the first thing the doctor says, cutting the tension in the room by half.

As he explains the exact situation and procedure, you take the time to look at Andrew. His eyes are closed in a peaceful sleep. His head is laid tilted away from you, so you can't see the area where he'd been hit. He's still wearing his suit—the shoulder now stained red, but his head looks as if it's been cleaned. His hand, still as it may be, is held away from his body with the palm up, as if he's still reaching out to you.

"Let us go then." Andrew's mother's tears seem to have finally stopped thanks to the knowledge that her son would be safe.

With her words, the doctor and his helpers begin to push the gurney once more, Andrew's family follow closely. You begin to trail after Andrew, too, but once again the hand of the nurse comes down to stop you.

"I am so sorry, but having too many people around him when he wakes up may be too much. I'll have to ask you to leave." The nurse looks sincere in her apology, yet stern in her denial to let you in. "Don't worry, he'll be fine. You'll just have to talk to him another time. Would you like me to escort you out of the building?"

You can't fight the hospital into letting you into Andrew's room, especially not when you're this tired, so you leave. Well, you try to leave. When you arrive at the main entrance of the hospital, you find a wall of security guards holding off a sea of reporters.

"Is Andrew Smyth alright?"

"What happened to him?"

"Is it true that he got hurt in a bar fight despite claiming to have gone sober?"

The paparazzi—who told them Andrew was here? Another patient, or a worker at the hospital maybe?

You suppose it doesn't matter, you were told to leave.

After spending some time getting past the guards, you try to squeeze your way past the paparazzi but get stopped as they hound you for information on Andrew. Before you can get out of the spotlight, an announcement comes over the hospital instructing you to "Please go to Room 480." So you turn around and fight your way back into the building, and make your way up to Room 480.

With how long you've been up, and this going back and forth, exhaustion is dragging your body down. After taking a deep breath, you enter the room. All eyes turn to you. The mother and two women are standing off to the side talking to the doctor and, most importantly, Andrew looks to you with a sleepy smile.

Again, like no time has passed at all, Andrew calls out your name and beckons you over to his side. His hand, though not lifting off the bed, is held open for you to take if you so do wish.

"How are you?" he asks, as if oblivious to the fact that he's the one on the hospital bed.

From this angle you can see the injured area, especially with the side of his head having been shaved almost completely clean of hair. There's a bandage covering one small section, the area they have most likely stitched back together. The painful image doesn't match his apologetic smile.

"I am so sorry for making you go through all this. I hope I didn't scare you too much," Andrew says. His breath is slow and shallow but peaceful, and his eyes are far more focused than the last time you had seen him. Despite this calm state, his brows curve as much as his tired muscles can in concern. "I understand that you may not want to bother with me while I'm stuck here, but perhaps, when I'm healed, you could consider giving me a second chance at that date?"

The End

CALL HIM

He went through the trouble of trying to find you, so he deserves a call at the very least. Besides, your friend is right on the basis that Andrew is being uncharacteristically interested in you, at least by his playboy persona standards. You sit silently as the phone rings in your ears; you breathe slowly in anticipation until it happens.

"Hello?" he answers, the simple sound of his voice swiftly brings up memories of that night. While reminiscing however, you notice that there's quite a bit of noise coming from his side of the call. Voices, dozens of them, and the clicks of cameras, sporadic yet never ending.

"Hello?" you repeat back. The volume of your voice naturally rises a tad as if you have to talk over the crowd. You give your name, hoping it will jog his memory. He repeats your name to himself before it quickly clicks in.

"You actually called, and so soon!" He is surprised, for sure, but it's clear your voice is a pleasant surprise, like someone receiving a call informing them they had won.

"I was worried you wouldn't, what with your friend saying—never mind. How are you?" He sounds so jovial, and the way he speaks is like a friend connecting after a week hiatus rather than a man you spoke to for just a few hours one night. He asks about things you had brought up in the lengthy conversation you had shared, like your day-to-day life and things you had been concerned about. The conversation occasionally swerves to him and his own life but the focus is very much on you.

You speak for five minutes, but it feels like an hour's worth of chatting. Then you're suddenly interrupted by a voice calling out to Andrew.

"How are you today, Mr. Smyth?"

"Fine, thank you, bu—"

"Is it true you co-directed this film?"

"I wouldn't go that far. I just suggested some things, now could I—"

"Is it true that you …"

And so on, you hear a barrage of questions aimed at Andrew. There are so many voices talking over each other that it gets to the point where you can't even make out the questions. You listen to Andrew trying his best to politely back away from the many conversations, and begin to wonder why he's being interrogated. Cameras click, and many of the questions revolve around a film—*oh, god.*

"Where are you?" you ask, just to clarify in case your suspicions are incorrect. There's a chance your question could have been lost in the numerous other ones, but instead Andrew's attention whips back to you.

"Oh, I'm at a premiere—but don't hang up!" he adds quickly, as if he knows you're considering it. "Please. Just give me a minute to answer some questions, then I can leave. I actually think this premiere is being live-streamed, so maybe you can look it up. Oh god, that sounded so conceited." The last few words come out like a whispered smack to his own forehead.

"You look amazing, who are you wearing?" The voices start again.

You sit there for a moment, listening to Andrew answering questions, politely yet not as calm as he usually does, before you decide to take his idea.

You look up the premiere that, like Andrew thought, is being live-streamed by several people. You peruse the different sources until you find one that is specifically streaming him. The frame rate and quality of the picture are decent, like you're watching a video recorded by someone's phone. Thankfully, the camera operator has made it to the front of the crowd, so even though you can hear the other reporters' voices and a handful of outreaching arms holding microphones, your view of Andrew isn't blocked.

With this new view on the screen, you can see how tense his smile is as he continues to hold his cellphone to his cheek.

"I see you," you announce, causing a visible shiver to run up his spine.

"God, that sounds so unsettling, even coming from your pretty voice."

Andrew's smile changes then into something far more genuine. "Which camera are you watching from?"

You direct him towards the camera acting as your eyes and ears. He smiles and waves at you subtly before turning back to the crowd, lowering the phone to his side.

Though he seems a tad happier with you watching him, he is distant compared to his usual behaviour. Andrew had always been so comfortable when it came to interviews, whether they were being broadcast live or filmed for later use. He almost always gave his full attention and respect to the people trying to talk to him. Right now, however, his smile seems forcefully stretched across his face. He stares at the interviewers like a student listening to their teacher after school purely because they feel like they have to, or risk receiving punishment.

Perhaps it's the stress of making a woman wait on the phone for him—maybe you should relieve him of that. He's on the red carpet trying to promote a movie while dozens of people are trying to talk to him at once, he doesn't need one more. Besides, you can always call him later if you want.

Then again, didn't he specifically ask you to stay on the line? Would it be rude to hang up on him?

Hang Up ⊙ PAGE 108
Stay On The Line ⊙ PAGE 157

CALL OUT TO HIM

Seeing as the man now ripping the sheets off the bed you just slept in is in no mood to cooperate, you take matters into your own hands. With a deep breath, you shout Andrew's name.

The man jerks back at your sudden booming voice. He turns to you, seemingly ready to yell back, but stops.

"Whatever," he mutters to himself. His tone isn't very convincing in his disinterest of you. Even so, he refuses to speak any more, though he does occasionally glance to see if you're still there.

You push him aside in your mind and focus on finding Andrew.

You call out again, this time you can hear your voice echoing off the tall walls of the living room. It seems like the home doesn't have a full second floor, but instead an indoor balcony that wraps around the whole home above the living room in a C-shape. As you shout out Andrew's name again, you scan your surroundings and consider the possibility that Andrew is upstairs. There are three doors up there but only two down on the main floor, one exiting the building and one heading back into the bedroom. It's not until the fourth call, when you hear a faint voice calling back your name, that you notice another set of stairs. They're tucked under the staircase heading up to the second-floor balcony, and head in the opposite direction. You call for Andrew again, just to confirm that you heard his voice coming from below you rather than above.

"I'm down here," Andrew clarifies, giving you enough reason to descend the fairly dark stairs. When you reach the bottom floor, however, the light returns thanks to a large glass door that leads out onto a deck. Andrew is sitting inside at a dining table. It's relatively large, able to seat twelve, and it's half covered in papers and home decorating swatches.

"You're still here," he states, rather than asks. An inky black brow rises in intrigue.

You explain your reasoning for seeking him out, and question who the man that had ordered you to leave was. Andrew listens attentively, but when you bring up the man his shoulders slouch and he lets out an exasperated sigh.

"That's Zach, he's a friend of mine. He cleans this place and does laundry and dishes. I pay him in room and board. I left a note telling him not to disturb you, I suppose he lost patience," he explains, rising from his seat and beginning to approach you. "Please don't think too badly of him, he simply has low tolerance for the women I bring home."

The implications of his words don't slip past you, but the sincere smile he flashes dazes you enough to let him speak first.

"I am happy you came looking for me, though. If I'm being honest, I was hoping you wouldn't simply walk away."

He takes your hand gently in his, holding you so softly that you feel as though you could slip out of his grasp if you don't hold your hand steady. The fact that you do makes his eyes soften.

"This may sound odd, especially considering the reputation I have," Andrew's gaze drifts for a moment, smile flickering before he turns back to you. "But I had a wonderful time last night. I understand if you are sceptical, but I would love to have the chance to take you on a date, a proper one."

His grip tightens a tad, as if to show his honesty through the light squeeze, though it's better represented in his eyes.

The End

CHECK OUT HIS WORK

You decide to see whatever project he's been working on, and Andrew seems positively elated.

"Then, please, come this way."

Without warning, Andrew grabs your hand and begins leading you further into his home. It's not the gentle touch like when taking you from the party to the limo, that shyness seems to have dissipated in the light of his excitement. What he's doing now is a proper grasp of your hand, fingers curled around yours like this was a casual date.

"And I feel like I need to apologize now, because I'm probably going to run my mouth like a revolving door for the next couple hours and—"

Andrew's fast pace slows, giving you a chance to breathe and take in the scenery. His eyes drift to the other side of the room.

"One moment. I just need to do something before I forget." He lets go of your hand so he can use his to reach into his pant pocket.

As you mindlessly follow Andrew across the room, you observe all the opal red colours around. The surrounding of red with yellow hue, along with the lighting, make it almost look as if you're surrounded in a gentle fire. The thin yet elegant design on the wall, the furniture, the rare decoration—they all look to be ablaze, like a warming campfire. The only thing that doesn't seem opal red-themed is the wall to your right that is a window looking over fields of crops, though you're far too high above them to tell what's growing there.

When you reach the other side of the room, you find Andrew has taken something from a shelf full of modern-looking decorative items. He's fiddling with it and you peek at his hands. He's holding a cheap-looking coin display case. He opens up the back, and fills one of the three empty spots with another colourful coin. Then he shuts it, placing it back on the shelf so you're able to see the discs fully.

They're Alcoholics Anonymous coins, trinkets you get from AA groups as a sort of reward for staying sober for a certain amount of time. There's three on display: 24 hours, one month, and the newly-added two months.

"Let's head downstairs then, shall we?" Andrew grabs your hand again and starts leading you away. It's clear he's not interested in discussing what those coins represent for his past, but you notice his eyes studying you, as if trying to gauge your reaction.

You follow Andrew back across the room and down the stairs; an excited aura fills the air around you two again.

Once you reach the bottom floor, it's as if you've stepped through a portal at some point during the descent. You've gone from a pristine, magazine photo-shoot-ready room, to a family's home. To be fair, what you're standing in is a dining room, but the decorations tell a different story. It's a mess, photos line the walls in non-matching frames, trophies and other such personal objects line shelves that wrap around most of the room. It's as if a family has been living there for centuries, with memories collecting over time.

"It's quite a lot, isn't it?" Andrew says, noticing your wandering eyes. "Most of my family lives in small places, and since they come here every week for dinner, they left all this stuff with me."

He starts to retrieve papers, a laptop and some swatches from a few different shelves, letting you peruse the room.

Having collected all he wanted, he asks for your attention. He had warned you about his ability to talk for a long time, and he wasn't kidding. For the next few hours you learn about his secret passion: cooking.

Since the age of eight, he explains, he's been helping his mother in the kitchen. He's learned everything from the women in his life, which has inspired him to start up a restaurant. Once open, he would still work as an actor, but manage the restaurant and, more importantly, create the menu.

Your conversation flutters between family stories, his indecisiveness in the decor, to some honestly useful cooking tips. Andrew's passion for the project is shining bright and constant throughout the conversation, which is admirable, but also a little too much for you to withstand.

You try to stay awake, you really do. But the clock strikes 6:30 a.m., and soon after you begin to fade. You try to keep up with his talking but it's no use, you're taking longer and longer to reply, until you stop. The last, fading thing you recall is losing the feeling of the chair under you, and being held against something warm, a light, rhythmic, pounding lulling you deeper into sleep.

You wake to the warmth of satin sheets draped over you. The room is lit by the afternoon sun, even with the thin curtain's attempts to block it out. You look to a clock sitting on a dresser to your left and confirm that it is past noon, and yet it's practically silent. A rare car passes outside, and then, of course, there're the noises you make yourself, but nothing else. For a long while you lay there, indulging in this feeling of being completely alone in the world, and that's why, when you finally hear another person's presence, you spring into alertness.

For a moment it feels as if your heart has stopped—similar to times when you're home alone yet think you hear movement. Once you're able to calm yourself, you take a minute to try and gauge what's going on just by sound. From the sound of shoes being dropped, to the rustling of a jacket being removed, it seems as if someone is entering the building after having been out.

In time you gather enough courage to slide out of bed and leave the room. You find that you're on an indoor balcony looking over the opal red living room you had seen yesterday. There's a door to your right and a door to your left, but you don't enter either of these. Instead you follow the balcony's C-shape until you get to the staircase leading down to the main floor. There you find not Andrew, but the roommate he had briefly mentioned.

The roommate looks to be in his late thirties, yet his brown hair is already starting to fade into grey. His clothing, while an average t-shirt and jeans, is very well maintained. They look fresh from the store, yet also broken in.

"Well, good morning to you." The man greets you once he finally notices you descending the stairs. "I guess I should explain first that I'm not a robber."

He approaches you carefully, hand extended for a shake. "Name's Zach. I keep this place clean, do the laundry, too. And you must be Andrew's new girlfriend, or at least that's what he's hoping for."

He gives you a playful smirk, like a college guy who knows they're messing with their friend but finding it too funny to stop.

"I gotta say, I was pretty shocked when I woke up this morning to find Andrew carrying around a beautiful woman like he had just kidnapped her from the party he had gone to. At least getting you into a bed was easy, what with him holding you like you were newborn kitten." He looks as if he's about to burst into laughter, but whether that's because of your reaction or Andrew's inevitable one, you don't know.

Out of curiosity on both parts, you and Zach start up a conversation, eventually migrating onto the opal red couches as you do so. He is rather eager to tell embarrassing stories about Andrew, yet also asks you quite a few questions. Eventually, after having tried to pry into your personal life a fair bit, you decide to ask why.

"I'm just super surprised, you know? Andrew hasn't really been the kind of guy to bring a girl home and not do her since a few years ago. Too many chicks using him as a jumping off point for their careers, acting or reporting—but then *you* happen. I gotta know what your deal is, why he thinks you're so special."

For a moment Zach looks content in what he said, but then his grin flips upside down. "God, that sounded super rude, sorry about that." He starts to fumble a bit, as if he's afraid of having possibly insulted you. "I better get to work."

He stands, his expression adding "Before I mess up again" to his spoken words. "You can head downstairs and cook yourself something if you want. I ain't much of a chef, so it's up to you. Andrew's probably not going to be up for another hour or two."

And with that, he leaves you to do as you wish.

Food does seem like a pleasant option, especially considering you were up all night without food and then slept most of the day. Focusing on your stomach seems to make it realize you're paying attention, and it gurgles at you like a whine from a child. Food suddenly sounds amazing, so maybe you should make some.

Perhaps you should make a lot so that when Andrew got up you could offer him some.

Then again, that might be kind of presumptuous. You don't actually know when Andrew is going to get up, so maybe it would be safer to just make enough for yourself. Not to mention cooking for a chef does have a shade of intimidation.

Or perhaps you shouldn't just walk into someone else's kitchen and start eating their food. It seems rude, especially considering he was kind enough to carry you to your own bedroom for the night.

But Zach said it was OK …

Don't Make Any Food ◆ PAGE 66
Make Enough For Just You ◆ PAGE 134
Cook For Everyone ◆ PAGE 44

CLOSE WINDOW

You sigh and slowly shake your head. Please, one girl's rejection has him chasing her like he's in puppy love, maybe even considering turning over a new leaf? More like his pride has been hurt. But you're not going to puff up his ego just because he's a little more determined than expected. You could explain your feelings to him on the situation, but will he even listen, or just try to convince you otherwise?

So, you turn your head away and roll up the window, not wanting to watch his expression fall as his manly pride gets a good jabbing. Instead you look to your friend who, though obviously shocked, does not comment on what just happened.

You're not going to let yourself be played by some guy who thinks he can get any woman he wants just because he's attractive and rich—you deserve so much more.

The End

CONTINUE CONVERSATION

You return the smile and decide to carry on with the conversation. The night is going more like you're good friends rather than like he's trying to get in your pants, so why start trying to get sexual now? At least not in the car.

The two of you chat lightly; a pleased grin on his face the whole way, his eyes glued to yours.

The limo comes to a halt after what seems like only a few minutes, but is maybe closer to twenty. Andrew is quick to jump out and proceeds to hold the car door open for you. You step out and gaze up at a two-storey house built atop a slow rise hill. The way the moon shines down on the pristine charcoal black paint gives it a mystical feel, like a mansion occupied by present-day, civil vampires. Aside from the uncommon black paint job, the building's style is modern yet generic in that way. The grass is green and well kept, though the front garden seems rather short compared to the building size. There is a clear, thick path going along one side of the house, showing that there's some form of a backyard.

"Like it?" Andrew asks. "I've actually been considering selling it, if you're interested. Even with a roommate, I always feel so lonely in such a big house." The smile he offers you is shy, like a newly-pubescent teen worried his attempt at flirtation would have the opposite effect. "Or perhaps you might be able to convince me to stay."

Andrew turns away from you after these words, cheeks turning red like ripening tomatoes.

Unable to say another word in this state, Andrew ushers you to the front entrance. He unlocks and opens one side of the double doors, holding it for you to enter first. You step into the small hallway making up the first area of the home; the ceiling is lower than an average room's height, yet just as large diameter-wise. You can see the end of the hall opens up to a bigger room, though you can't see much of it. The only part you can see from your position is that at the other side of the room there are a set of two staircases, one going up and one going down. You don't get too far into the hallway though, when a phone interrupts the quiet night. You look to the device making the noise. It's a stationary phone that's been designed to look like a rotary phone but more modern; the numbers aren't holes in a circle but buttons instead. It's sitting on a long wooden desk with some useful knick-knacks such as writing utensils and a notepad.

"I am so sorry, but I need to take this." Andrew's smile is sincere as he slips past you. "I'll try to be quick."

He picks up the phone and answers pleasantly despite the interruption, an advantage of being an actor, perhaps.

"My, you're calling late… Urgent, how so? … Really? … That's wonderful! I—" Andrew's eyes fall back to you and a bit of his excitement fades. "I would love to hear more, but I've got someone rather special visiting right now." He turns his red cheeks away as his teeth lightly bite down on his lower lip. "I think she might be … I hope … Could you email it to me? … I'll see you then … Goodnight."

Andrew hangs up the phone, a giddy smile plastered onto his face with no sign of coming off anytime soon.

"That was about a personal project of mine." He points down at the phone. "I've been working on it for months." He looks to you. "Would you like to come downstairs and see it? Well, what I have so far anyway." There was a slight pause while you think, which he interprets as you maybe not being interested in the offer. "Or … do you have something else in mind?"

Do you? Have you perhaps been harbouring the craving for something more intimate? Perhaps all this time huddled beside each other talking, part of your mind has been drifting off into something a bit more scandalous.

Or would you rather keep things innocent. You two are having fun without taking your clothes off, why start getting dirty now? Besides, he just looks so proud and excited to show off his personal project. Does the relationship really have to be cemented in a bed?

Check Out His Work ➲ **PAGE 35**
Ask For Sex Instead ➲ **PAGE 16**

COOK FOR EVERYONE

Why not cook a meal for everyone? Andrew has been so kind to you, and Zach is already getting to work, a meal is a simple way to say thank you. Besides, maybe you can even impress Andrew with your cooking—if that's possible with his level of experience.

You head down the stairs into the room you had passed out in that morning. You don't spend too much time there as you beeline for the set of double doors and swing them open to reveal a restaurant-grade kitchen. It's not just the utensils and equipment that are prepared to serve a lunch rush, but there are also multiple ovens, a walk-in freezer, a fridge and a cupboard that take up the rest of the floor. It's kind of exhilarating—having all these options and all of this space to make whatever you wish. You get to cooking, letting your creative mind run free like a child on the playground.

It seems like your creations are coming out well as Zach and Andrew come wandering into the kitchen, following the scent of cooking food.

Andrew catches sight of the food you're cooking him and listens to the way you greet him. These things seem to spark something in him, making his curious expression melt into something akin to blissful contentment, like a man seeing his wife holding their baby for the first time. For a while he's a bit dazed, soaking in the feeling of having you, Zach and him eat together.

Once you're all finished eating, the boys swoop in to clean the dishes for you, but Zach pushes Andrew out of the job pretty quickly.

"You two should hang out while you have the time," Zach says, smiling at Andrew like he's the actor's wingman.

"I would like that, if you don't mind, of course." Andrew smiles down at you, having taken up the space so close beside you that your arms can't help but brush against each other. "Perhaps I can show you around my work, introduce you to some of my co-workers."

Andrew's co-workers, as in other movie stars?

"But you have the day off. You really wanna go to work when you don't have to?" Zach asks, turning to look at you guys but still holding his dripping wet arms over the bubble-filled sink.

"I don't mind, it's not like I'll be working. Besides, she said she liked my work, correct?" Again Andrew looks to you, it's as if his eyes aren't able to stay off you for long. "I thought it would be an exciting experience to have you see a little more into my world."

"Showing off the perks of being your girlfriend, huh? I think that's bribing."

"Zach!"

Zach bursts into laughter, Andrew fumbles over his words, attempting to get his friend to stop. As they chat, you have some time to consider Andrew's offer.

A private tour around a movie set. How would Andrew introduce you? If you were to go off of what Zach is implying …

The sound of your cellphone buzzing snaps you out of your thoughts. The boys all look to you as you look to your phone to find that the responsibilities of life have come knocking at your door.

You can't just go running off a second night. You have responsibilities to take care of like everyone else in the world. This was all definitely fun while it lasted, but for now you should go home.

Don't Go To The Set ⊙ PAGE 62
Go To The Set ⊙ PAGE 100

COOK WITH HIM

"Really?" Andrew's tired face lights up in childlike excitement, one foot rising behind him as he leans over the railings a tad more. "I'll get started while you come up here and change." He disappears quickly back into one of the rooms without giving you time to say anything more. You make your way upstairs and find Andrew already descending them.

"My room is the first door, feel free to put on whatever you like." Andrew flattens himself against the wall, allowing you to pass first.

Once you reach the second floor, you get the feeling there's eyes on you and so you turn to look back down the stairs. You see Andrew still standing there, his dreamy expression jumping in slight shock and his already pink cheeks darkening to a light red.

"Sorry."

He doesn't run off right away though. He continues to enjoy the sight of you for a few more seconds before backing away, eyes staying on you as long as they can.

You continue to his bedroom, where you find something comfortable of his to wear. When you leave the room, you run into Zach who offers to wash the clothes you had just removed.

"I'm an expert at this stuff, so don't worry about me wrecking them." His confidence exudes out like a fog, especially when you agree. "And thanks, for doing this with Andrew," he adds. "I haven't seen him so happy in a while, I was starting to worry about him."

He leaves you with that, and walks past you to enter the last room in the row.

You make your way downstairs, back to the dining room full of memories. Instead of looking at them, however, you follow the sound of books—it sounds like someone is switching between several of them. You push your way through swinging double doors and find Andrew hunched over one of four cookbooks laid out on the table, one of which being the one he wrote. He looks up when he hears you, but doesn't say anything right away. He stares, mouth falling open only to close and make a bashful smile.

"It's been a while since I've had a woman wear my clothing, though none have looked so adorable." Andrew's eyes dart away for a moment out of embarrassment, something he hadn't done last night at the party. How does he go from calm flirtation to blushing like a middle-schooler?

"Anyway, I have some ideas … for cooking. But I'd love to hear any suggestions you have. I'm willing to follow your lead, which ever you like."

The End

DANCE

The smile he gives you has a cocky layer to it, like he knew that you would answer as such.

"Sadly, I must admit that I'm not actually the best dancer. I hope you don't mind a simple hug and sway." The grin he wears, and his slight squint give off the air of a not-very-subtle lie, like he wants you to know that he would make any excuse to hold you close.

Nevertheless, you lay your hand atop his, signalling you both to stand. After helping you up, he moves his hand to the small of your back and leads you to the dance floor. Slowly but surely people start to notice the two of you—well, more specifically Andrew—and attempt to approach, only to be given a quick greeting from Andrew before you move past. It's like black and white how they treat Andrew with such warmth, trying to get his attention like he's some sort of fabulous prize to be won, but only look at you in passing with confused expressions.

Despite the attempts and intrusions, you get to the centre of the dance floor where the most eyes could be on you. Despite this, Andrew's attention is fully on you as he pulls you into an embrace. His left arm snakes around your waist and he pulls you tightly to his chest. You barely have time to situate your own hands before the next song begins.

Slowly, you both start to sway back and forth. You try to watch Andrew, who wears an almost mischievous grin, but your eyes keep drifting to all the people around you; they're watching and whispering to each other.

You rest your head on his chest, partly to avoid the judging eyes. As you press against him you can feel his warmth wrapping around you like a blanket, feel his breath against your hair, and just barely hear his heart beating.

"You see them ... all these people looking at us?" he asks. "You know why?" He leans in so his lips practically brush against your ear as he whispers. "They're all regretting not having snagged you first." His hands dip a tad lower, though respectfully still stay at your sides.

Soon, the music stops, giving you the opportunity to pull away from him. He flashes a self-assured smile at you. His mouth opens as if he's about to speak, but a man approaches.

"Mr. Smyth, good evening." He greets the actor with an outstretched hand, barely sparing you a glance. He's slightly shorter then Andrew, about six feet, and looks to be double his age. He wears an old-looking grey suit and a salesman's smile.

"Evening, Mr. Finster." Andrew accepts the handshake. His smile looks sincere, though his free hand wraps around your waist and pulls you close, as if trying to silently point you out to the man.

"How are you?" Mr. Finster asks, yet doesn't give Andrew time to respond before moving on. "I was hoping we could chat about that business venture we were discussing last week," he continues, making it blatantly obvious why he came tonight.

"As interesting as that sounds," Andrew says, releasing Mr. Finster's hand so he could make a gesture towards you. "I have already promised this lovely lady a drink."

Both men look to you, one with a raised eyebrow in scepticism and a slight threat, and Andrew with an almost pleading smile. Having suddenly been thrown under the bus, you are left to decide the fate of the actor's night.

You could save Andrew from a night of boredom and take his sudden offer for a drink—this may be your chance get to know him on a more personal level.

Or you could take this chance to make a graceful escape. There is still a possibility that his intentions are just as your friend had warned. Do you want to risk being another woman in his bed?

Escape After Dance ➲ **PAGE 72**
Save Him ➲ **PAGE 144**

DECLINE DRINK

Again, you reject it, finding his persistence rather odd and a little pushy. It gives the idea that maybe he has some sort of end goal.

His expression falls again, though this time it's more annoyance than shock. Andrew lets out an exasperated sigh, palms coming to cover his face, hiding his expression. It's sudden but, to be fair, it would be rather frustrating to be continually rejected. Eventually he peeks at you and notices you're still sitting there. His eyebrow juts up in intrigue, his hands slide down and curl into a fist with his pointer finger and thumb resting atop his lips.

"Have you heard the rumours about me?" he asks, smiling like he was about to tell a dirty secret.

You nod, assuming he's speaking of the rumour that he always arrives alone yet leaves in company.

"Well then …" His grin becomes rather playful and his eyes drift down slowly then back up. He slides the side of his leg up your inner calf. "Why don't you come to my place and discover the truth for yourself?"

It's such a sudden turn in his demeanour, but if the rumours are true, the offer isn't out of place. You suppose he's confirming them, but you're still left to give an answer.

Does it excite you, the idea of running off with a celebrity for a single night of pleasure?

Or are you put off by his offer, the destruction of your romanticized vision of this man making it hard to be aroused?

Or, are you frankly insulted by this man thinking that a few compliments give him the right to ask for sex? Does he think you're that easy?

Go Straight Home With Him ◆ **PAGE 89**
Politely Decline ◆ **PAGE 141**
Slap Him ◆ **PAGE 150**

DEMAND HE TALK TO YOU

This was bull. You've been trying to speak to him since getting into the car, at the very least he could ask you to leave himself rather than shoving the duty off on someone else.

When you express your desire to speak to Andrew, the maid looks annoyed, like you're a nagging child.

"Talking to him isn't going to accomplish anything."

Any form of friendliness from the maid seems to have been thrown out the window.

This man's rude and dismissive behaviour paired with how Andrew had treated you only serves to increase your anger.

You demand again, this time in a harsher tone which gets a reaction out of the maid. He leans away from you, eyes growing in shock yet still with an air of annoyance.

"Whatever," he sighs, spinning on his heel and marching out of the room.

You hear his footsteps go a ways away, then up some stairs, then above you before eventually stopping somewhere on the second floor. If you listen very closely you can barely make out a pair of voices, though what they're saying is beyond you.

After about 10 minutes, a car pulls into the driveway. You hear a heavy set of footsteps get out of the car, slam the door shut and enter the building. When the footsteps reach the bedroom and the door swings open, it's not Andrew standing there. Nor is it the maid. A man with muscles bigger than his scowling face stares you down like a spider torturing its prey by making it wait to be eaten.

"Mr. Smyth wants you to leave," he says in a voice smooth like James Earl Jones, yet still threatening.

You suppose this was Andrew's response to your request.

The End

DEMAND TO SEE HIM

You can't stand this. This man was rude enough to barge into the room, not giving two cents about the fact that you were naked, and demands that you leave. Well, you have demands of your own. You fight back against the man's rudeness with anger, his expression turns sour, like you're just some drunk bum nagging him for money. For a moment it looks as if he's going to reject your request but with a shrug and an indifferent "Whatever," he leaves to get Andrew, apparently finding you not worth arguing with.

You take this brief moment alone to get dressed, and that's all you have time for. Just five minutes later, Andrew is standing at your door, arms crossed in a closed off stance.

"Hey," he says dryly. He's not rude, but accepting the fact that he's going to get yelled at. "I'm not sure how many times you've done this, and maybe it's coming as a shock to you, but this is the part where you leave." The kindness in his voice is gone, and now there's just exhaustion of both kinds. "I know Zach was kind of rude. I've told him not to bother cleaning the sheets until they're empty, but he thinks the faster he gets all his work done, the more free time he gets, so, sorry about that."

The apology may have been nice, but the implication that Zach, the man that had woken you up, had kicked several people out of the very bed you just slept in is a bit unsettling. I guess being with you was just not that special to Andrew, you're just another notch in his belt, so to say.

"But … I'm not going to offer you anything other then a cab ride home."

The End

DO NOT LEAVE PHONE NUMBER

What's the point? Grasping at straws won't do anything but stretch out your hope and fertilize the painful feelings inside of you. You're not the first woman to go home with Andrew just to sleep with him, and you won't be the last. The least you can do is not bother him any further.

The walk home is long, but it gives you time to think, to accept your feelings and start to grow past them. When you're back in your personal space, a feeling of comfort washes over you like an embrace from a loving parental figure. You make yourself some food and snuggle into warmth.

Your relaxing afternoon takes a bit of a hit, however, when you start browsing the Internet and find the latest scoop:

"Another Night, Another Woman For Andrew Smyth"

You read a short article about Andrew's womanizing nature. Thankfully, it focuses on him rather then the person he had taken home, though the article does express some curiosity in who the woman was. There's one picture attached to the news, a shot from the back of Andrew looking down at you as he leads you to his limo. Your face can't be seen; you're just a figure of a woman walking alongside Andrew.

The End

DON'T GO HOME WITH HIM

You find your balance, stand straight, take a step away and decline the offer. You were having such a good time together, why did it have to end with you going to his home?

Andrew stares at you for a moment, smile still painted on his face as his eyebrows curve as if he's not sure how to feel. Your friend is still standing beside you; she's clearly confused but has two fingers pinching your clothing, ready to pull you away if needed. Eventually an awkward chuckle breaks through Andrew's stunned state.

"Sorry, that was a little forward wasn't it?" He seems to be grasping for straws, or maybe just thoughts. "How about something a little lower key, I know this nice restaurant nearby. I haven't eaten since brunch and from what I've seen leaving the kitchen, it doesn't look too appetizing. What do you think?" His smile is shaky, like he doesn't want to show anything else.

It seems like he is being a tad pushy, and that was a rather quick change from basically asking if you want to sleep with him to "Let's have a cozy little dinner together." Or is that being too sceptical?

Whether an oddly quick change in plan or not, it's dinner. It's not like he's going to try anything, and it would give you two more time to talk. Maybe it would be fun.

Go Eat With Him ➡ **PAGE 80**
Don't Eat With Him ➡ **PAGE 58**

DON'T CALL

You close your phone and place it down nearby.

You can't, you have this gut feeling that it's too good to be true. There has to be a catch somewhere, but you don't want to find it. It's better to get out now before you get hurt, it's the safer option.

The End

DON'T EAT WITH HIM

The speed at which his sexually-laced offer changes tone, turning into a supposedly innocent dinner practically gives you whiplash. So fast that it just doesn't seem possible, so you politely decline again.

A twinkle of hurt is hidden behind Andrew's confused eyes, a forced smile coming to aid in the strong facade.

"May I ask why?"

Should you be honest, lay your feelings on straight and think, or sprinkle it on gently?

But you don't get a chance to choose as your friend, trying to help, gently grabs your shoulders.

"She's not really interested in one-night stands," she says kindly as she begins to lead you away. You have just enough time to look back once to see Andrew slide down onto the bar stool. His expression is solid and blank, like he's trying to process something internally without letting it seep out.

As the two of you are driven home, your friend explains how she thought your hesitation to answer was you freezing up—she was trying to help. The honesty in her apology is clear, or maybe it's her acting ability being shown off. Either way, there's no point in arguing as you're already a long way from the party. Whatever you have left to say to Andrew seems like it will have to be kept to yourself.

For the next couple weeks, that one night drifts from a dream come true to a simple dream. Maybe the people that brushed off your claim of having danced with a celebrity as "Too crazy to have happened!" is getting to you. A seed of doubt sinks into your brain and grows with each normal day. It's not until a little under a month later that your Cinderella night swoops back into reality in a rather unrealistic way.

A padded envelope, as long and wide as an average sheet of paper, arrives at your home. Inside is a note and another envelope, this one of thick, glossy white paper. It's lined with gold filigree on every seam and has a reflective stamp holding it together at the back. Before opening it, you look to the handwritten note that has your name at the top.

> *I hope this reaches you, as your friend was not as cooperative as I had hoped. She was rather hostile, claiming I had bad intentions. After she explained her reasoning, I now understand her scepticism, and possibly yours. I see that I did not fit your—*

You could see the word fantasy hidden behind a hasty scribble of pen.

> *—-image of me, and so may have upset you in some way. To be honest, you are not the first person to be disappointed by how I actually am, but unlike anyone else, you didn't leave. And like you stayed to speak with me that night, you have stuck in my thoughts since then. Though I cannot tell you why this is happening, I can decide to do something about it. With this note comes an invitation to this year's Metta Charity Event. If, by some miracle, you have been thinking about me as I have you, you could consider coming to the event as my date. If not, if this is simply me beating a dead horse, then feel free to throw this all away, that is your prerogative.*
>
> *I hope to see you there.*
>
> *-Andrew Smyth*

Your eyes fall back to the gold-lined envelope, now aware of its contents. Whether you do something with its contents is your choice.

Do you go to the event? Show up to see a guy that claims to have fallen for you after only a few hours? It sounds like a romantic movie or fairy tale, like it just isn't true.

Then again, it's not like this was some elaborate prank, Andrew never seemed cruel enough to do such a thing. And to send you such a note that had most likely been written and re-written countless times, and an illustrious invitation such as the one you have, this seems to be too much for anything other than the feelings he claims.

Go To The Party ➲ **PAGE 97**
Stand Him Up ➲ **PAGE 153**

DON'T GO TO HIS HOME

You decide to decline the offer, suspicious of his sudden desire to whisk you away to his home. The night seems to be going well, but perhaps once a player, always a player.

Surprisingly enough, instead of having an expression that showed a man's pride being suddenly jabbed, Andrew wears one of a guy being rejected.

"Oh, alright then ..." His voice drifts off as his eyes lower to the counter in thought. Before you can decide whether to just get up and leave or not, his gaze floats back to you, a shimmer of determination sparkling in his smile. "Can I walk you home at least?"

His persistence could be sweet, or based in stubborn pride. There's no real way to tell, but it's up to you to choose.

Will you let him have this, a chance to make amends? He is trying to be sweet, hopefully, so why not let him escort you home? No harm done, right? It's not like you have to invite him in.

Or is it still a little early to be showing him where you live? You've only known him for one night, it may not be safe. Speaking of being safe, did he say "Walk you home"? Walking around at 2 a.m., just the two of you ...

Go Home With Your Friend Instead ➡ **PAGE 86**
Let Him Escort You ➡ **PAGE 126**

DON'T GO TO THE SET

The world seems to fall silent when you say this. For a while, Andrew just stares, the hope in his eyes dripping away almost into tears. The sound that eventually breaks the uncomfortable silence is Zach who continues with the dishes, eyes purposefully avoiding you and Andrew. This sound seems to rattle Andrew back into being able to respond, though it sounds forced, along with its calm delivery.

"That's … alright. It's getting dark though, may I escort you home?" His expression doesn't hold hope, but a vague desperation, like he's stalling for time.

You feel overwhelming pressure to let him walk you home, and so you do.

It's almost unbearably awkward as you two leave. Andrew doesn't even seem able to find the drive to change out of what he'd slept in. You leave his home and begin walking; the two of you exchange the smallest of sentences as you navigate the dimming roads.

Andrew looks awfully tense and keeps his hands to himself as he looks off into the middle distance, his mind clearly calculating something. It's almost fascinating the way his expression is changing, like you're watching a movie on mute, trying to deduce what people are feeling solely through their expressions and actions alone. From nervousness, to hurt, to fear, Andrew looks like he's choosing which person to save from a burning building. Eventually his inner debate seems to end as he lets out a shaky sigh and looks to you.

"Can I ask you something? And please be honest." Even with a determined expression, his voice is shaky. "I'm sure you noticed at least a few of my attempts at flirting, so is this—is wanting to go home … a gentle way of rejecting me?"

Was it? This was all a magical night, but an exhausting one. He's a famous actor and soon-to-be a restaurant owner. Could you keep up with him? Could you handle dating a guy who is staking his life so high with responsibilities?

Perhaps you could. Or maybe you couldn't, but you could try, for Andrew.

It Was A Gentle Rejection ➡ PAGE 111
It Was Not A Rejection ➡ PAGE 112

DON'T LOOK FOR HIM

Having snooped around the seemingly empty home and stumbling onto something so personal, you start to feel rather uncomfortable, so you take your leave.

You don't write a note or any such thing, leaving nothing to show that you've been there at all. The walk home is long and tiresome, but you march forward until you arrive in your comfortable and familiar space.

You try not to think about Andrew and his home as, even if you grow any regrets in the future, there's nothing you can do right now; but the thoughts come barging into your mind anyway about a month later.

Your friend, the one that had brought you to the party, sends you a link to a YouTube video. It's of a convention panel featuring Andrew and a few of his co-stars from the movie that he had just starred in. Along with the link, your friend points out a specific time to watch in the video, so you skip to that. It looks like fans were coming up and asking questions to the stars, and the one you end up skipping to is of a teen girl who shakily approaches the microphone that'd been placed at the end of the middle walking strip between the chairs. They ask her her name and she bashfully tells them it's Tasha.

"I, um … know this might sound kind of stupid but, I—I just thought I'd ask you how you were all doing. You know, how's life?"

You can hear a couple of the other guests snickering, possibly at the question or Tasha's troublesome shyness, but the stars were open to answering. A couple of the stars even pointed out that it was a unique question and that she was kind for asking, which helped grow Tasha's confidence, even if her pink cheeks darkened to a red.

The stars took turns answering the question, giving brief little descriptions about their current lives; one woman talked about having to spend the weekend with her sister while she was in labour, and another about having trouble with the playful kittens that his cat birthed a couple months back. But it's Andrew's answer that you focus on the most.

"I've been alright, I guess," Andrew says, fidgeting in his seat, his already shaky smile falls a little more.

"That ain't true," says the man beside him, slapping the back of his hand against Andrew's arm playfully. "You've been moping around forever, man."

Some of the other stars seem to agree, one even asking what was "up" with Andrew's mood. Andrew tries to wave off their concerns but soon breaks down and hastily admits, "There was this person I met recently. She was an amazing woman, and I was kind of hoping for something special with her, but it didn't work out that way."

He keeps his eyes down, trying to keep a smile on his face.

"You were rejected?" the man beside him asks, seemingly flabbergasted that Andrew could be turned down.

"I suppose so. She didn't say it directly, she just walked out on me."

The End

DON'T MAKE ANY FOOD

Barging into someone's kitchen and using their food without their direct permission just isn't something you can bring yourself to do. So, instead you're left to find a way to entertain yourself. Going snooping around his house isn't really something you're interested in either, so you find a comfy place to sit atop one of the opal red chairs and wait.

You have your phone on you, and Zach is kind enough to give you the Wi-Fi password, so you're able to keep yourself entertained for a while. Long enough for Andrew to find you.

"Good evening," he smiles down at you from the indoor balcony. He leans both his forearms onto the railing like a lovesick romantic lead watching his crush walk by. He's wearing sweatpants, his feet and chest are bare. His eyelids seem heavy though; there's crescents resting under them like he hadn't slept as well as his body needed. "Zach tells me you haven't eaten."

Your eyes dart to Zach momentarily as he carries a bucket of water up from downstairs, the grin on his face cheeky as a preteen getting away with their first swear word.

"It's getting late again, I know a good restaurant nearby."

"Or you could cook something, Mister Chef." Zach yells up to his friend, though Andrew can't see him from his position.

"You just want me to make enough for you too," Andrew retorts, leaning over the railing just enough so that he can see Zach who looks comically offended.

"Excuse me, but I was just thinking that maybe you and the lovely lady could have a cooking date." Zach rolls his eyes so hard it must have hurt as his nose pointing up to the sky. "Plus, I'm hungry," he mumbles, making both himself and Andrew chuckle.

"Aside from your ulterior motive, it actually doesn't sound like that bad of a plan. What do you think?" Andrew looks back to you, smile growing from one of tired curiosity to a sense of innocent bashfulness as he begins shifting from one foot to the other. "You can put on some of my old clothes so you don't wreck yours and we could cook together." Andrew seems to notice his rising excitement and quickly tries to dampen it. "Or, if you don't want to work, we can still go to a restaurant."

You've had such a hectic past 24 hours, just sitting back and letting someone else do the work does sound nice. Not to mention the way Andrew's body is slouched, as if begging to lie down. You both could use a break.

But being able to see Andrew doing something he loves, witnessing that proud excitement you had glimpsed yesterday while he was describing his cooking experience, what a sweet memory that would be. And Zach even pointed out that it would be a date, an unconventional date, but most likely a fun date nevertheless.

Go To A Restaurant ⮕ PAGE 91
Cook With Him ⮕ PAGE 46

DON'T RISK PUPPY LOVE

You decide it's not worth the risk of having it fall out from under you in a week or two, and so you decline. His expression drops not to simple sadness, but to a more knowing, dejected smile; he hangs his head, his gaze falling to the ground.

"I understand, sounded kind of silly didn't it? My apologies." His disheartened tone conflicts with the shaky, smile on his lips. "Anyway," his gaze snaps back up to you, a forced cheerful grin on his face. "I should be heading home."

He takes a few steps back as he speaks. "You have a good night, hope to see you around," he says as he turns and takes his leave, moving at a brisk pace.

It's not until the next day, when you receive a text from one of your friends saying that he had had an "epic drinking contest" at the local pub, that you find out what Andrew did with the rest of his night.

The End

DRINK

Well, it seems much more fun than sitting alone sipping water all night, so why not? You order a beverage of your choosing as he starts a conversation.

It's a bit awkward at first, what with the lifestyle difference you two are in, but it doesn't take long for you to find a sort of common ground—difficulties with certain kinds of people, school and childhood stories, things almost everyone on the planet has had in some capacity.

After the initial kick-off, everything seems to roll along rather smoothly, like the two of you have been friends for longer than a couple hours. The only bumps come when he flirts with you. Most of the time it's subtle, occasionally to the point where you're not sure whether to consider it a flirtatious act or not, but a few times it's spoken with such confidence that you're a bit thrown off. It's not that the conversation comes to a screeching halt whenever he drops a compliment, but it's a sudden shift in atmosphere which carries through the night.

You're able to relax as time goes on, but there's this nervous edge that hangs over you.

One thing that, surprisingly, doesn't change is Andrew's attention on you. Even when the other guests inevitably realize he's there and approach with a warm greeting, he politely acknowledges them then arranges another time to chat as he is currently occupied with you. It's oddly sweet, especially when beautiful women, some you even recognize as actresses and models, approach and yet are cast aside for you.

Some leave with a polite smile, others raise their noses into the air as if to insult you both, and one man and his female companion even make a passing joke that Andrew is shooing them off because he's not interested in a threesome that night. The comment seems to come out of nowhere and, though the couple laughs at their own joke, Andrew only offers a dry chuckle, looking a bit annoyed behind his smile. Is it because he doesn't want you to feel awkward, or is there a little too much truth in the joke than he wanted?

What an unsettling thought: that this conversation would be merely a means to an end. Yet he rarely makes any sexual passes, let alone touches you. Ninety percent of the flirtatious comments are more on your personality rather then your body, and even when your body comes up, it's usually about how beautiful your eyes are or something to that effect. Andrew, in general, keeps his hands to himself. He is being much more appropriate than most would expect, at least with how the media paints him. Maybe you shouldn't judge a book by others' reviews.

As you two chat, time speeds by around you, turning 7 p.m. to 12:30 a.m. And you may not have noticed if it wasn't for your friend calling your name as she taps your shoulder.

"It's time for us to g—gooooo." Her voice turns silky smooth as she notices Andrew. "Sorry to interrupt." She looks down at you with a smile that screams her excitement, and intoxication level—but that's more of a backup singer.

"It can't be that late already," Andrew says, more to himself than to you. He looks up at a nearby clock. "Wow, time does fly when you're having fun, I suppose," he remarks turning back to you.

You go to stand from your seat at the bar where you've been parked for a couple of hours. Your legs feel a tad numb after not being used for so long, but he stops you with a simple, "Hey."

"I had a good time tonight," he says with a rather sincere expression. "And no one said that just because the party is over it means we have to stop hanging out."

One of his inky black eyebrows rises slightly as he glances at your friend to see if she will protest what he's suggesting. "Why don't you come over to my place and we can chat a bit longer, what do you say?"

What do you say?

Being invited to the home of a celebrity seems like the best-case scenario for a lot of people. Think of what could come of it: a relationship, or a pure friendship, or even a sleepover. It could be any of these, or it could be just one—the last one.

He is known as a womanizer—even by his friends, if you are to consider that one couple that made the threesome joke. Besides, it's past midnight, how much longer can you both stay awake for?

Go With Him ➔ **PAGE 103**
Don't Go To His Home ➔ **PAGE 61**

ESCAPE AFTER DANCE

Your friend's warning about Andrew's womanizing ways flashes through your mind. You take a step back and say something along the lines of not wanting to interrupt business.

"Ah, smart woman, thank you," Mr. Finster says, his grin rises contradicting the fade of Andrew's hopeful smile.

"Now, come, Smyth." Mr. Finster places a hand on Andrew's shoulder and begins leading him away from the dance floor.

Andrew doesn't struggle. He simply keeps his eyes on you, not like a friend would when stabbed in the back, but like a man who'd done something wrong yet unsure what he actually did.

You try to mingle with the other guests but find very little success. You spot Andrew amongst the crowd every now and again, always stuck in a conversation that makes his charming smile stretch into one of frustrated boredom. There's a brief moment where his wandering eyes catch sight of you, and his dull, glazed over eyes light up. He tries to walk in your direction, but the woman speaking to him grabs his arm, making him look away just long enough for you to get lost in the crowd.

Eventually, the night ends with you and your friend getting into a limo. The loneliness caused by the other guests' disinterest in you weighs you down with fatigue. As expected, your friend had an eventful night, dancing and chatting with various people while avoiding a couple perverts. She leads the conversation, pulling it along until she's interrupted by a tapping sound.

It happens about 10 minutes into your trip. Your limo slows to a halt in front of a red light when you hear a string of three taps. At first your friend keeps her eyes on you, a single brow raised, then she catches sight of something behind you and they shoot up.

"Oh my god." She hastily grabs your shoulder and tries to turn you forcefully, but her shock and refusal to take her eyes off the oddity make her push weak. You shift in your seat though, so you face the door on your side.

There, just outside your closed window, you see Andrew leaning most of his upper body out of a limousine window. His fisted hand uncurls so he can give a casual wave, as if he wasn't hanging out a soon-to-be moving vehicle on a busy street. He points downward, signalling you to roll down your window.

"Good evening, ladies," Andrew offers a smile portraying his understanding that the circumstance was odd, but urging you to play along with it. He gives a quick nod of acknowledgment to your confused friend before focusing on you. "My apologies for the intrusion, but I was really hoping to talk with you more."

Your limo jerks suddenly as it begins to move forward. Andrew pulls back into his quickly-fading car and yells up to his driver. "Keep up with the car beside us."

He leans back out of his window, though not as far as before, and the wind catches his hair and tie, throwing them around lightly.

"I understand this isn't the best place for conversation," Andrew says. He tries to chuckle casually but it comes out stressed, like a man nervous to ruin his first date, "but not being able to find you, then having been told that you had left ... it—scared me into taking, arguably absurd, action."

The limos suddenly jerk to a stop at another red light, snapping Andrew back to the dangerous circumstance. "I doubt we can keep this up for long."

Andrew looks back to you suddenly, his shyness getting pushed aside for the moment in exchange for determination and worry. "Perhaps we can meet up somewhere, just you and me?" He reaches a hand out to you, the tips of his slightly shaking hands reaching into your car. His voice becomes a tad weak, like he was afraid to say them at all. "What do you say?"

Wait, does he mean—a date—right now? As in *tonight*?

You can take the offer at face value, grab his hand and climb into his car. Screw laws! If he is willing to hang out of a moving vehicle to talk to you, why can't you jump into his car while it's moving? Use the liberties of fiction.

Or, you could be safe and just shake hands, maybe agree to park somewhere so you can switch vehicles. It's definitely the less sporadic and crazy option, and perhaps he was actually hoping to schedule a date some other night. It *is* roughly one in the morning.

Or you could stick to your guns and close the window. How could one dance change a famous womanizer? There's no way, you won't fall for it. Maybe this is just his stubborn, cocky pride that made him chase you out of a party. Would you be OK with this if any other man did it?

Switch Cars ➔ **PAGE 161**
Shake Hands And Make Plans ➔ **PAGE 147**
Close Window ➔ **PAGE 40**

FALL ASLEEP

You push aside Andrew's abandonment. You're far too physically and emotionally drained to put up any sort of fight, so you let your mind drift away to a kinder place. Unfortunately, you're dragged back a handful of hours later when you're woken up by a cold hand shaking your arm.

"Hey, get up. Time for you to go home."

Your mind begrudgingly accepts the turn of events and you come to realize that the person waking you up is, in fact, not Andrew.

"Come on, I need to clean the sheets by tonight," the man complains, brushing his fading brown hair away from his eyes. He looks to be in his late thirties and very unhappy with how long it's taking you to get out of bed.

Eventually you rise and take a moment to look around the floor for your clothing. Instead you're pointed in the direction of an opal red laundry basket.

"They're in there." Comes the answer to the question you didn't ask.

The man seems unfazed by your naked body; he doesn't even look your way as you gather your clothing. He is so calm despite the nude woman standing in the room, like he'd gotten over the shock of it long before you ever came to the house.

You throw on your now-clean clothes and your curiosity begins to grow. Eventually you ask the man who he is.

"Call me the maid of this place. I clean, I take care of the garden, I get room and board. It's a pretty sweet gig," the maid says, his smile more innocently friendly than anything Andrew had given you. "Do you want me to call you a cab or something?"

It seems like a kind gesture, or perhaps it's a hint that you should hurry up and leave. Your business here is technically finished.

Everything offered has been done, so there's not really anything left for you to hang around for.

Then again, isn't it a bit rude that Andrew hasn't even had the common courtesy to ask you to leave himself? Is it too much of a bother for him, so he's sent his maid to do it, like some sort of pompous rich lady who doesn't want to deal with people?

Is this worth getting upset over though? You could always leave a message with the maid before you go.

Demand He Talk To You ➲ PAGE 53
Give Message To Maid And Leave ➲ PAGE 79

GET BACK IN THE CAR

"Get lost!"

"Oh my god!"

"You god damn—"

All the voices are getting to you. You can't handle all this negative attention, and so you react under pressure. You tell him to go back to his home and hastily get back into the cab. Your driver seems to need no words from you and speeds off, leaving Andrew standing alone, barefoot and shirtless in the street watching you go.

The End

GET UP AND GO HOME

"No, it's not. In fact, I was just leaving."

You're done for the night, burnt out by the solitude and awkward attempts at conversation. You stand from your seat and begin to walk away with the intent of finding your friend and informing her that you will be leaving first.

"Oh, well, have a good night," the man stammers, obviously taken off guard. You leave him there without a sparing glance and make a beeline to your friend who you could, thankfully, spot with in the crowd. She was still speaking with her superior, so you use it to your advantage. Interrupting them for only a moment, you announce that you're leaving and then slip away again, giving her no chance to question you unless she abandons her conversation—which she could not do. It's a bit underhanded but having her trying to convince you to stay doesn't sound fun.

You take a taxi home and the ride flies by without incident, aside from a couple concerned texts from your friend. Soon enough you're back home. You change into more comfortable clothing and sigh in relief, feeling like you can finally relax.

The End

GIVE MESSAGE TO MAID AND LEAVE

Starting a fuss doesn't seem like the best option, especially considering how thrown off Andrew seemed when you had tried to start a conversation. Giving him some space seems like a good idea.

But, a small, wishful part of you doesn't want to give up all hope quite yet. Before leaving, you ask if the maid could deliver a message to Andrew for you, the hopeful part of your heart cracking a little when the maid looks humoured by your attempt.

"Sure," he says with a shrug of his shoulder. The maid pulls out his phone, clicks a few times, then gives you the go-ahead to start giving your piece. His fingers go fast, typing almost as fast as you speak. He doesn't need you to pause; your slightly slower speech is enough to keep him following you.

With your message and contact information given, the maid gives a sigh and lowers his phone.

"I'll be sure to give it to him," he says. He grabs his now-full laundry basket and starts to roll it out of the room, his continued talking pulling you along with him. "But I gotta be honest with you, he's not going to get in touch with you."

He stops, letting the cart wheel forward a bit while he stays standing beside the desk. "Not that there's anything wrong with you. He just doesn't really double dip on one-nighters, you know?" He offers a kind smile, as if apologizing for his employer's actions and his correct prediction.

The End

GO EAT WITH HIM

Though the invite to his home still reeks of an attempt at a one-night stand, he does look sincere in his apology and offer for an innocent meal. Besides, you couldn't afford the outrageously expensive entrees the party had offered, so, an invite to dinner—albeit a very late dinner—is welcome. Giving him the benefit of the doubt, you agree to the 2:30 a.m. dinner date.

"Wow, don't *I* feel loved," your friend accentuates her words, placing the tips of her fingers on her chest.

"I'm sorry," Andrew apologizes straight and deadpan, with a smile just as cheeky as your friends. It's pretty clear that he doesn't intend to invite her as well—not that she really wants to come (though she will definitely be asking for all the details tomorrow).

"I'll be taking the limo then. I trust you can take care of her?" Though some may see the basic implication of her wanting Andrew to get you home safely, the piercing eyes she shoots at Andrew give a hint that her question has several more layers.

"With all my being, as long as she lets me," Andrew says, turning his gentle gaze to you and offering a smile. You're unsure if you're supposed to respond verbally or not.

"Alright then." Your friend looks from you to him, taking note of the fact that she's no longer in the eye contact circle. "Call me if you need anything," she tells you, eyes still watching Andrew. "Have a good night you two."

Finally, she quits the scene, leaving you with Andrew's unwavering gaze.

"Shall we?" He waves his hand in the direction of the door, giving you the opening to start walking. You turn and start to head for the door; Andrew comes up on your right side. For a second you can feel fingertips brush against your lower back, but they dart away soon after.

"Sorry," he apologizes out of the blue, left hand grabbing his right wrist behind his back, as if to hold it there. "If I'm being honest, I don't know very many places open this late, so is a family-style restaurant OK with you?"

Was there really any other choice outside of fast food?

You agree, and walk to his car continuing a pleasant conversation, but it's obvious he's trying to keep some distance. You keep seeing him glance at you, as if he wants to try something but refuses to. At this point on a date, someone would usually have put their arms around someone else. Then again, Andrew had attempted to hold you before and you had pulled away.

Thankfully, the physical barrier doesn't seem to affect the emotional connection you're making with him. By the time you're walking into the restaurant, you two are freely talking about personal opinions.

"Even so, I feel bad for all those smaller groups that get bad names because of a couple bad apples in the orchard." Andrew holds the door open and lets you pass through first.

The restaurant is decently large, able to seat about 80 people, yet only four tables are occupied. A young man sitting in front of a laptop and surrounded by books is sitting against a wall with a charge cord disappearing under the table. Near the bathroom are three people, two men and a woman, who most definitely look like they'd been consuming more than the food offered at the restaurant. Six men, four of which are wearing camouflage army suits, sit talking at the largest table with the largest pile of empty plates. Finally, there's a young couple, late teens, on a date gauging by how they're holding hands over the table. They notice you—or, more specifically, Andrew—right away.

You're approached by a tired-looking, college-age student who initially gives you a basic greeting.

"Good early morning. Thank you for choosing—"

The intake of air the young man takes is so strong you'd think he was suffocating.

"Oh my god! Andrew Smyth—I am a huge fan!" His eyes fall on you. His excitement freezes as his brain tries to conjure a reason for you being there. Eventually one comes to him: "Sorry, to interrupt your date. Would a booth by the window be alright?"

He gives a shy smile as he grabs a pair of menus. He walks you to your table and leaves you with your waitress.

The two of you sit across from each other with you facing the door.

"I kind of hope you like this place," Andrew says as he picks up his menu without looking at it. "I used to come here all the time with my mom and sisters."

He smiles nervously, as if he's hoping you'll find his comment cute rather than weird. "Fun fact: that half of the restaurant used to be a play place."

As he points out how the restaurant has changed over the years, and tells some rather comical stories, you feel something warm rub up against your leg. It disappears rather quickly, replaced by Andrew's questioning gaze, his eyes watching you with nervous hope.

"Can I have your autograph?"

Andrew nearly jumps back in surprise, but he's able to turn to the girl with a smile—one he's probably practiced for years with paparazzi.

The woman in question ends up being the teen. Her date stands beside her with a measly sheet of paper compared to his girlfriend's school binder.

Andrew hums long and slow, giving him time to look over at you.

"I'm kind of in the middle of—"

"Come on, it's two signatures. It'll only take a minute." The girl slaps her binder down on the table and points her pen at Andrew. Her other hand rises and grabs the paper out of her boyfriend's hands who looks almost embarrassed by his partner's actions.

"Alright then." Andrew gives in to the demand; the teen would have probably bullied him into doing it anyway.

Andrew quickly scribbles down his signature on both items and hands them back. The teens give a smile, one more apologetic than the other, and return to their seats. As you and Andrew continue your conversation, the two pull out their phones and start tapping away.

"I'm sorry about that. I can't seem to get away from it."

The warmth returns to the side of your leg, starting at your ankle and slides upward to your thigh.

"I hope you don't mind it too much, because it will probably happen a few times a week—assuming you stick around."

The flirty talk seems to float around that level. His hope doesn't rise too high, his wariness of pushing too hard being linked to your rejection of going to his house. But his interest is still shown openly, as if in offering.

Unfortunately, your date is crashed by a group of seven teen girls peeking their heads into the restaurant. A worker tries to approach them, but they wave him off, pointing at the table where the teen couple is sitting. They wave at each other, and the girls run over to them. They don't even sit down, but instead exchange hugs with the girl who points them in Andrew's direction.

At this point, Andrew notices them. After an exasperated sigh he looks to you with a sheepish smile. You can't even give any sort of blessing before the group of girls walk up to your table.

"Oh my god."

"You're Andrew Smyth, right?"

"You were so hot in *The Spring We Came To Life*."

They all start talking over each other, even nudging one another in an attempt to get just a bit closer.

"Can we take pictures with you?" asks one.

"Alright, but if we could please make it quick." Andrew waves a hand towards you, smiling apologetically.

"Oh yeah, of course," the girl that had asked assures him, but her friends are not as kind. One rolls her eyes, a couple look down at you and sneer like you were attempting to flirt with their boyfriends.

Andrew looks as if he's about to stand but, instead, a girl shoves past the first girl and slides into the seat beside him. He's obviously taken aback by the action, even more when the girl tries to lean against him. Andrew, actor smile still on his face, leans away from the teen and lets her take the picture.

While he's occupied with the photos, you're left to look around silently and eat. You study the girls out of boredom, noticing how their outfits are a little too fancy for 3 a.m. Their makeup had been painted on thick and fast considering how uneven it was. Their skirts are high and their collars low. They'd probably been woken up by the excited texts of their friend over there on the date. You imagine how the girls had raced out with the chance of meeting a hot celebrity pounding in their hearts. Maybe they thought they could have a Cinderella night, and didn't care that he had already found her.

The round of pictures starts coming to an end and, unsurprisingly, some start pulling out books, pens, and one even grabs a paper napkin.

"Could you sign my diary?"

"I don't—" Andrew starts.

"Me too, me too!"

"And me."

In the distance, you see two girls and two boys pop into the restaurant. Before a worker can approach them, the guy on the date stands and calls them over.

God, does it ever end? Is this really how you want to spend your night, sitting silently, being ignored as your date gets way too much attention. Can't Andrew tell them to piss off? You shouldn't have to deal with this, you can just leave.

Then again: it's not Andrew fault. Even the fan's actions are a bit understandable, especially considering you went to a party in hopes of meeting Andrew. Plus, this couple's friend list can't go on forever. It will end eventually, right?

Leave The Restaurant ➡ PAGE 120
Tell The Teens To Buzz Off ➡ PAGE 168
Stay Until He's Done ➡ PAGE 158

GO HOME WITH YOUR FRIEND INSTEAD

You can't. It's too early in this relationship—if you can even call it that—to have him coming to your home, whether he entered or not. Getting driven home with your friend is a much safer option—but you don't tell him that outright.

You politely reject his offer, and see a quiver in his smile.

"Alright then … have a good night," he says in a tone that half-heartedly tries to hide his dejection. Whether he's doing this because he really feels hurt or because he's trying to guilt you isn't certain, but either way you stand from your seat. You give each other light, goodbye smiles before you follow your friend. He doesn't chase you out or anything, but, as you would find out around a week later, his thoughts most definitely followed you.

The next week you're sitting at home without much to do when you get a call from your friend. After a few pleasantries, she tells you what brought on the call.

"I just got off the phone, actually, with the one and only Andrew Smyth." She teases you like you're teens talking about a crush.

Then her tone dips into an *Oh my god, can you believe it*-explanation: "Apparently he looked through the guest list and Googled all the names, but couldn't find yours 'cause you were my plus one, right? But he found me, so he called my agent, who called me, then *I* called Andrew and he wanted to call you. I didn't feel comfortable giving you number out without your permission, so I took his number and said I'd pass it along," she explains. "I'll text you the number. And I must say, he's being uncharacteristically interested in you, you know. I haven't really heard of him doing this for anyone else—but that's just me." There's a sheer-thin layer of regret in her voice, but she doesn't speak it.

The phone call ends soon after with her pushing you to call him *immediately*. Not even a minute passes before you get a text with

Andrew's number—your friend claims it's his personal phone. You sit, staring at the number for a while before you receive another text from your friend. This time she admits to being on Andrew's side, having heard his supposedly-sincere voice when he asked to speak to you. It's clear that her opinion of him has shifted dramatically, but has yours?

There are so many claims of his womanizing. To have him throw that out after one night of chatting with you, it seems unrealistic, does it not? Can a couple hours really influence him that much?

Maybe it can. It's a sweet gesture, and one that would take a fair bit of work for just a fling. Maybe he's not the player the media claims him to be.

Call Him ⮕ PAGE 30
Don't Call ⮕ PAGE 57

GO LOOKING FOR HIM

It doesn't seem right to just abandon Andrew like this, maybe even more so after finding out this fact about his life. It's obvious he's not in the living room, so you peek into the small hall that has the front door at the end of it. You look outside and into the one room protruding from the hall which turns out to be a guest bedroom. You don't find Andrew, so you decide to head downstairs.

As luck would have it, you find him still sitting at the dining table, but no longer working. His head lies on the table, his cheek pressed on top of the spine of the cookbook he had written. His mouth hangs open ever so slightly as he breathes quietly; his eyes are closed, but his curved brows give him an upset look.

Suddenly Andrew shifts, groaning out in pain as his sleeping expression shifts into one of discomfort. Unfortunately, he doesn't escape the painful plastic spine, and it leaves a red dent across his face. In his shifting, he shakes slightly, and curls further into himself, though it doesn't look like he gains any more warmth. Even in his sleep his brow is curved in frustration, but it seems to be too little to wake him.

You shouldn't leave him there like that, his sleep would be practically useless, and when he does wake up, he'll only be in pain. Unfortunately, you can't lift him, at least not without shifting him around to the point where you would wake him up, so what should you do?

The least you could do is try moving the book out from under his head, and perhaps you could find a blanket around to drape over him. Would that be enough though? Perhaps you should simply wake him up so he can move himself to a place he could lay down.

Tuck Him In ➡ **PAGE 177**
Wake Him Up ➡ **PAGE 179**

GO STRAIGHT HOME WITH HIM

This is a once in a lifetime opportunity, something thousands of people would fight for a chance at. Why not take it?

When you agree, Andrews smile turns almost wickedly devious.

"Let's not waste any time then." Andrew stands from the bar stool and extends a hand to you, his movements are so smooth you could mistake this as a scene in a romantic movie or a James Bond film.

Most party guests glance over at you as you walk past. Their reactions vary from yearning to aggravated jealousy. Having people watch you, wanting to be you—it's not a sensation people often get to feel.

Along with all the eyes watching, you can feel Andrew's hand on your lower back, fingers spreading and closing so that his pinky slides over your rear then pulls away so his interest isn't so obvious to others. This continues until you reach his limo outside.

You exit the party out of a side door, away from the paparazzi. He opens the limo door for you and you slip into the back, the velvet-like seats assisting the slide. Andrew gets in after you and a reflective piece of glass at the far end of the seating area slides open, revealing the driver side of the car. The driver is a man, a bit older then Andrew, with an amused-yet-knowing smile on his lips.

"That was fast," the man comments, smugness pours out towards Andrew at the level that only a friend could get away with. Andrew doesn't seem fazed by the comment, and just scoffs subtly to himself. The driver turns his eyes to you just long enough to give you a once over before looking back with a slightly different kind of smile. "Well done."

Andrew smirks at the comment but says nothing in response. The driver closes the window, creating a little private room for you and Andrew, who immediately tries to get to work.

His hand comes down onto your closest knee; the tips of his fingers are so cold it makes you flinch. He continues to hold your leg despite your slight discomfort with the temperature. He moves smoothly, but not slow and sultry like fans imagine him to be. It takes under five seconds for his hand to go from your knee to the top of your thigh, fingers reaching for your core.

He's obviously not leaving any time for you two to get to know each other, and considering how most one-night stands end, this might be your only chance to talk to him.

Then again, you didn't get into this car with a claim of friendship.

Try Talking ◆ PAGE 176
Just Sex ◆ PAGE 113

GO TO A RESTAURANT

"That's alright," Andrew says, trying not to look disappointed, but some slips through. "It's been an awkward night, sleep patterns thrown off." It's not devastation, just that his preferred option was not picked, but he accepts it. "Since you're still dressed for the party, how about we make it a fancy night out?"

Andrew leaves your sight and disappears into one of the rooms on the second floor.

This time Zach says nothing. He simply scoffs to himself and continues on with cleaning. You sit alone for another 15 minutes until Andrew descends from the stairs, now sporting a three-piece formal suit. A fake white rose sprouts from his breast pocket to match his white bowtie.

"Come, I've already made reservations." He offers you his elbow, then leads you out of his home. There's a cab waiting for you two in the driveway as if it had appeared out of thin air just for the two of you.

The restaurant Andrew takes you to is a place called 8 Bells. It's quiet and a live piano player plays what sounds like a lullaby. There were about nine tables in the whole place, each seating only two. They're spread out at least 20 feet from each other and filled with refined-looking men and women who seem content to enjoy the music without the need for much chatter. The lights are dim, giving you just enough light so it doesn't hurt to look at others.

Like a stereotypical gentleman, Andrew pulls out the chair for you before taking his own. He lets out a long sigh when he sits in his chair, his shoulders slouch forward like he's finally resting after a marathon. Andrew lays his hands in his lap, his eyes close as he sways gently to the music.

"Calming, is it not?" His eyes flutter open so he can look at you, his smile like a man wakening up to his wife sleeping by his side, still tired, yet willing to stay awake just to watch you. "I must thank you for allowing us to come here." His voice is soft, so as not to disturb any of the other guests. "I didn't realize how much I needed a break until you gave me the opportunity to have one."

His gaze slowly sinks to his lap, his smile turning to one of a man accepting his faults. "I tend to over work myself, only realizing I have when it's too late." His eyelids slide shut again. "But I feel comfortable relaxing with you. I don't feel like I have to force myself into taking a break." You feel his legs reach out for one of yours, not to rub up against them, but to hold one between his like he would your hand. "I just naturally slow down and enjoy the moment with you."

The End

GO TO HIS HOME

You agree, lifting your head to look up and see his almost-smug expression. He helps you stand up straight, but one arm stays wrapped around you, holding you close like you might to try run.

"Follow me," he instructs you, giving your friend a quick glance as if asking for permission, however, it's obvious he's going to do as he likes no matter her response.

"Use protection," she says, glaring at Andrew. The words are a joke but her voice sounds spiteful. "Call me if you need anything," she adds just as you lose sight of her.

Andrew walks you to his limo, head held high as people watch you two leave. You're able to catch a couple comments about Andrew's womanizing and assumptions on what you two would be doing tonight. Andrew says nothing about them though; he starts up another conversation, purposely asking for your attention.

Eventually you reach his limo, and, after assisting you in getting in, the conversation ends. It's not that you ran out of topics, it's just that Andrew seems finished speaking. He sits there, watching you with such intensity you're sure he's mentally undressing you.

Clearly, he's found a way to entertain himself for the ride home, but the silence is not as entertaining to you. You study his eyes and find they do currently have a devious nature to them, so why not indulge in it with him? A little appetizer before you arrive at a more suitable place for the main course ...

Or is that going a little too fast? Jumping from chatting to foreplay is rather sudden. Not to mention you're not exactly in a private area. There are dozens of people outside the vehicle that could peek in and spot you, including the driver of the limo that, though currently out of sight, did have a sliding glass window where he could easily look in. It's risky, so perhaps you should just continue the conversation for now.

Talk With Him Instead ❥ PAGE 163
Start Getting Sexual ❥ PAGE 155

GO TO THE PARTY AFTER TRYING TO STAND HIM UP

The guilt weighs down on you until you break. You may arrive late, but you just can't leave him there waiting for you.

You rush through any preparation you need to do, making mistakes that eat up your time because of it. It takes so much longer than you want it to—hours even, with the fixing of slip-ups and the travel there. By the time you finally arrive, you don't have to push through paparazzi, but the guests leaving the party instead. Weaving through people to make it into the ending party, you spot Andrew sitting on one of the steps leading up to the front door and freeze.

His eyes are glazed over as he stares down at a rose he's holding in his lap, twirling it slowly as if trying to keep his attention on it rather than his own thoughts. You walk up to him carefully, putting on a gentle smile as you quietly call his name. Slowly, he raises his head to look at you and, for a moment, he simple stares, as if his brain is trying to process who you are. Eventually he stands, wobbling slightly.

"Sorry I'm late," you say, but judging by the way his eyebrows momentarily jump up, it seems you both know why you're late.

"Yeah, well." Andrew takes a slow breath. His eyes try to connect with yours but drift away each time. "I'm happy you came, I just don't know what to think after having been left waiting so long." Again, Andrew looks down at the rose in his hand, not offering it to you, but instead focusing on it to think without the distraction of you.

He's so quiet, setting up an awkward silence that's hard to penetrate. The MC of the party is the one to break your silence.

"Alright, all you beautiful people that have stuck around till the end. You've been an amazing audience, but I got to head out, so this will be our last song," he announces. He receives a short round of applause from the remaining guests.

The clapping fades out and a slow, sensual song with light vocals starts to play. There's not too many people around, and those who are are quietly focusing on their dancing. The song is easily heard from where you and Andrew stand outside. He hadn't looked up when the MC spoke, and doesn't seem to care about the last song, so he goes back to his silent thinking without even looking at you.

With the word "last" echoing in your head, the factor of a time limit pressures you to act. Without being sure what to say next, you hold out your hand to him. He looks down at your palm, then at your face sceptically, a single brow raised in question. You offer a smile, and, after a moment of hesitation, he smiles back. He places his hand in yours and lets you pull him close.

The End

GO TO THE PARTY

People say that love is a magical and crazy thing, and this might be your chance at it. Even if love isn't what this is leading to, what a wonderful experience it will be. However, there's one thing that is most definitely horrible about this decision: the wait.

The party is another month away, which means you have the note and invitation taunting you for weeks on end. They seem to sit there, egging you on, like the countdown to a birthday. It builds your anticipation to an annoying level. It's not like you can talk about it with anyone, aside from your famous friend that took you to the first party, and she is almost constantly busy. Anyone else you tell would get jealous and even aggravated if you kept going on about it, so you're left to count down the days yourself.

Twenty. Fifteen. Ten.

Five, four, three, two, one! It's here!

The night of the party is upon you, and some of your excitement turns into nerves. They're not so bad that you can't make the party, though it is most definitely nerve-wracking to walk up to the security guards blocking the velvet-roped entrance.

After weaving your way through the crowd of people and cameras, you walk up to a long, half circle staircase leading up to the building. Two security guards stand at the end of a cleared path that you hadn't been able to access before. As gracefully as you can, you exit the crowd and step onto the cleared path, approaching the two guards. Without saying a word they look at you sceptically, arms crossed over large chests in a threatening stance. The seemingly impenetrable pillars softened, however, when you hand one of them your gold-lined invitation. One even gives you a smile as he unclips and pulled back the rope.

"Have a wonderful evening, madam."

You give a short reply as you pass by them. You put your invitation away and hear a flurry of clicks and shouts from the paparazzi. At first you ignore them, perhaps someone famous arrived just after you, but soon you realize that they're trying to catch *your* attention. You look up at the sea of flashing cameras, a bit like a deer in headlights, as people tell you to turn this way and that way, to smile or to pose. You're stuck in the spotlight, alone, doing your best to appear nonchalant, until someone arrives to relieve the pressure from the paparazzi.

"You made it!" Though happy, the amount of shock in Andrew's voice is almost sad. You turn to find him making a beeline to you, not fazed by the camera flashes and shouting in the slightest. A skill learned by most stars, or so your friend had told you.

"You came … thank you, so much." Andrew pauses, staring at you, his smile slowly growing. It's as if he's internalizing the fact that you're here, and what that choice means. In this moment, while he silently looks at you, the cameras seem to get louder.

People, dozens of people; many that are broadcasting to thousands more. While still in your trance, Andrew snaps out of his and suddenly holds out both hands to you.

"I got you this." Held between his two clasped together and slightly shaking hands, Andrew offers a single rose. "I considered a full bouquet but thought that might be a bit troublesome to carry around all night. Unless you're here with your friend." His hands retract. He looks to the ground as if his suspicions were fact. "I saw her come in."

You try to wave off his fear, but it may not be convincing what with your eyes occasionally wandering over to the paparazzi. They're calling to you by your hair and dress colour.

"Are they scaring you?" Andrew asks with a tilt of his head, motioning towards the paparazzi. "They can be bullies." He holds out his elbow for you, his smile a bit more confident than when you first arrived—but only a bit.

"Shall we?"

The End

GO TO THE SET

This is possibly a once-in-a-lifetime experience, your responsibilities could take a rain check for one more night. Your world wasn't going to fall apart because you took a bit of time off to indulge in some joy.

The moment you agree, it's like you've been whisked off on a prince's horse, everything seems to go so quickly. You are taken upstairs, you are led out the door, you are getting into Andrew's BMW—it's all going so fast, you nearly get whiplash. And all along that ride there's Andrew, smiling away and talking to you.

When you arrive at the set, which turns out to be a high school, the sun has gone down. They are filming in the gym, which has been decorated to look like a dance was going on. There are many people around, some in everyday clothing while others are wearing beautiful gowns and tuxes. Extras, Andrew assures you as you swerve through them. After exiting out into a hallway, you make your way to a classroom where you meet some faces you recognize.

Stars from various things you've seen are lounging around a makeshift break room in gowns or tuxes, and almost all of them stop to gawk at you and Andrew. Within minutes you're sitting at one of the chairs with all eyes on you. Questions fly at you like you're the first boyfriend to be brought home to the family. Thankfully, it's a bit easier to handle with Andrew standing beside you, a calm hand resting on your shoulder.

It's not until their break is over and they're all ordered to go back onto set that you finally get time to breathe.

"Sorry about that," Andrew apologizes again, this time his voice a mere whisper because, even though you weren't in the same room, they had started filming again. He kneels down beside your chair, his hand lying gently upon your leg. "We've all gotten quite attached to each other, having spent the last three years together filming this.

They didn't overwhelm you too much, did they? I can ask them to back off if you want."

"Not that we'll listen." As if on cue, in walked one of Andrew's co-stars. She had only given you her first name—Vanessa—and you don't know much about her. This is her first job in film, so you only know the few things she has told you. She claims to be a writer, acting only because she writes herself into all of her stories as an Easter egg of sorts. She was very kind when speaking to you before, hyperactive and curious, but kind.

"Do you ever listen to anybody?" Andrew jokes, his smile showing something akin to brotherly friendship.

"I'll listen if people will explain their reasoning to me. If you just barge in and try forcing changes onto my things, I'll get pissy."

Andrew chuckles, clearly knowing something you didn't, before turning to you. He looks as if he's about to say something but Vanessa interrupts him.

"Oh—the director wants to talk to you about re-shoots, by the way."

She looks directly at Andrew, her expression hidden from you. It may be intentional as Andrew seems suspicious.

"Which scene?" Andrew asks, as if turning into a detective for just that moment.

"The one where Guy starts beating on Lucas because he hurt Max," Vanessa answers back immediately. It seems to be just enough proof for Andrew and he stands slowly.

"Alright then. I'll be right back, OK?" Andrew looks to you with an apologetic smile as he backs away. "I'm so sorry about this." And with that, he leaves the room.

Vanessa kicks into gear, suddenly rush to your side.

"I gotta show you something real quick before he gets back." She pulls out her phone and, after clicking on a couple things, shows you the screen. "Look what Andrew texted us before you got here."

On the phone is a text message conversation, but Vanessa points to one singular word bubble. It reads:

I'm coming to the set today with a guest and I am begging you all to act appropriately. After showing her around, I'm hoping to ask her out.

The End

GO WITH HIM

This is an offer many people could only dream of getting and you aren't going to miss out on the opportunity. You agree to go with him, which makes his lips turn up in a smooth smile, but you can see excitement behind his veil of concealed calm. You look over at your friend who assures you "It's alright" with just her expression.

"My car should be just around the corner," Andrew says. He stands from his seat and, after a smile to your friend, offers you his hand.

You can hear your friend trying to suppress her giggles as you take it, but she fails. Andrew doesn't seem annoyed, however, if anything it's as if he's flattered; his cheeks pinken at your innocent contact. She continues to watch as you two leave, but does not follow.

Andrew doesn't pull his hand back after helping you up. He holds it out, palm open and up, with yours lying atop it like one would at a ball in years past. His fingers twitch, as if wanting to close around your hand but he holds his urge back.

An almost awkward silence falls over you both as you exit the building; a limo pulls up.

"Perfect timing." Andrew walks over to the car and holds the door for you, yet still keeps your hands connected as long as he can.

Once you seat yourself inside, Andrew, instead of moving to get in the other, spacious, side of the limo, slides in beside you. You fumble slightly in your attempt to move quickly aside to give him enough room to sit. Once seated, he calls to the driver that you're ready to leave without giving you the opportunity to make it to the other side of the backbench.

As the vehicle pulls away you slide back into an awkward silence. You hadn't expected to be sitting only a few inches apart while the other half of the backseat was left empty. Would it be rude to move now? Then again, do you really want to? Apparently Andrew didn't.

Just as the silence is beginning to get a tad too awkward, Andrew's knee brushes yours and he gives you a gentle smile. It's not so much a suggestive grin, but more like a comforting smile. The silence still hangs over you two, but the pressure is rising. It seems like Andrew is waiting for you to make the next move.

You two were having a nice chat before, and he invited you home to hang out, so why not start up another conversation?

Or, if you think he still has naughty intentions towards you, you could always get a bit of a head start. He must have sat this close for a reason, so why not take advantage of the lack of space, maybe even get a little closer?

Continue Conversation ➲ PAGE 41
Try Starting Foreplay ➲ PAGE 170

GO WITH HIS PLAN

You let Andrew walk closer, and closer, and closer still, until your back is pressed up against the wall opposite the desk. He places his one forearm beside your head.

"Are you OK with this? I won't force you," Andrew says, proving his point by opening up the other half of his body so you could slip away if you wish, but you stand your ground. His smile, instead of becoming smug at your submission into him, softens, as if he had a thought that you would leave.

"Well then, this way please." Andrew gestures his arms towards a door not too far from your position. "And I must apologize, but I will need one more moment." He leaves you to proceed to the next room by yourself as he returns to the desk.

You see him start to scribble something down on the notepad before you enter a dark bedroom. Instinctively you switch the light on, revealing a pristine guest bedroom, decorated, but not with anything personal. You get a few minutes to look before Andrew steps in, the actor takes a moment to stick a piece of sticky note on the outside of the door before closing it.

"Now that that's there," Andrew turns to you with open arms, "where would you like to start?"

It's not the smoothest transition there could be, but it does get the two of you started.

For the first few minutes you don't touch each other, just talk about what you want to do. Andrew walks around the room, gently touching things as he describes what he would like to do with you— to you. The suspense builds, and eventually you both break.

The night progresses slowly and Andrew is sure to do everything you two had spoken about. The talk of your gentle caresses takes longer than spontaneous movements, but that doesn't make it unenjoyably slow. If anything, the gentle touches cause you to react just as strongly as rough play; constant pressure and lack of breath being replaced with sudden spikes of pleasure and sharp intakes of air. All the build-up makes the finale that much more satisfying as well, and your journey out of consciousness so much easier.

When you wake up later that afternoon, after having fallen asleep at around 3 a.m., you find the bed colder than before. You stretch out from your position but don't feel any sign of another body being there. In your own time, you rise up from the bed and prepare to leave the room.

When you do leave, however, you come face-to-face with a man. He leans on the wall beside the door, closed eyes snapping open to give a glare as sharp as snake fangs.

"Took you long enough," he snaps, as if you should feel bad for sleeping as long as you did. He looks to be in his early forties, with brown hair that was steadily fading into a gray.

"Alright lady, time to get on outta here," he waves towards the door like you're a fly getting too close to his food. "I got laundry to do." He doesn't wait to watch you go, but simply pushes past you to get into the bedroom.

You're left standing in the small hallway in the front of the house. It was all so sudden that you stand there for a couple minutes, considering what just happened and what to do next.

Should you just leave as you've been—to be frank—ordered to? Considering Andrew couldn't even be bothered to ask you to leave himself, it seems he has no interest in interacting with you any further.

Do you feel like he should though? The night you had spent together was more than just sex, so at the very least you deserve to talk to Andrew, rather than being shoved out the door by some man who's now stripping the bed of its sheets.

That being said, the man looks far too annoyed to deal with anything, so asking him Andrew's whereabouts would probably get you nowhere. Having seen the home from the outside, it seems like the building is no larger than two stories, so calling out to him was sure to get his attention—but do you really want to wander around someone's home yelling their name?

Call Out To Him ➡ **PAGE 33**
Leave As Ordered ➡ **PAGE 117**

HANG UP

You decide it's best to hang up and let him focus on his job that you've unintentionally interrupted. You lower the phone to your lap and end the call.

Once you hang up, the room suddenly feels uncomfortably quiet, the lonely atmosphere sinks in like a heavy fog. You continue to stare at the screen separating you and Andrew, watching him cling to the cellphone he thinks you're still connected to. Eventually he decides to make his escape, backing away from the crowd as he raises the phone to his ear.

"I am so sorry, this is really important, I have to take it," he says just before turning to walk away.

Unfortunately, he's able to get far enough away so his words can't be heard, at least not by the camera. You can still see him speaking into the cell though; his footsteps slow until he stops moving altogether. It seems as if he finally notices you've left. He pulls the phone away from his ear and checks the screen. For a moment he simply slowly lowers his arm, the disappointment creeping in like a sunset. He ignores the various people calling out questions about his personal phone call, when he suddenly perks up.

He turns to you, or at least to the camera that you are watching through.

"Is this camera still live?" he asks the camerawoman who gives a nervous yes. "Hey, are you still watching?" he asks you, as if you could respond. "I hope so, because there's something I really want to ask you."

The End

HAVE HIM COOK FOR YOU

Andrew's face lights up like a kid being told they're going to a fair. He jumps out of the bed and quickly opens up two of the dresser drawers, pulling out fresh underwear and pyjama bottoms.

"This will be great. I haven't gotten a chance to cook for someone other than Zach in so long. Do you have any allergies I should know about? Just to be safe." Andrew listens to your answer, taking a mental note of it. "I'll go get that started then. There's a bathroom through that door if you want to use it." Andrew points to the second door that you had noticed last night. "And feel free to put on any of my clothing. I'll have Zach wash the things you wore last night."

Andrew moves and speaks with an enthusiasm that you've never seen him do on talk shows or the like aside from a few select moments of behind-the-scenes footage from some of his work. He practically skips out of the room, leaving you to prepare for the morning however you see fit.

When you do exit the room, you find Zach leaning on the indoor balcony railing.

"You all done?" he asks, hand reaching out to grab the handle of an opal red laundry cart. You let him in, and as he passes you he asks you a favour: "Don't worry if you can't eat it all. I usually have to transport all the extra food Andrew makes to the homeless shelter nearby. Just try to taste a bit of everything, OK?" He doesn't offer any further explanation but gives you an encouraging smile and a pat on the shoulder as he passes by to get inside the bedroom.

You go down to the living room but don't find Andrew. Instead you smell a heavenly scent coming from downstairs. You follow your nose to a dining room, fit to hold 12 or more people. There's a sliding glass door against one wall that not only has a beautiful landscape view, but a large deck that has yet another table where you could sit people down to eat. The room has a lot more of a personal touch, what with a variety of framed pictures, certificates and even trophies in various places around the room.

After a look around, you follow the scent of baking to another set of double doors, these swing open when you push against them. Inside the room is a restaurant-grade kitchen, state of the art equipment that is currently stuffed with bowls and trays of not yet completed food. Andrew is hard at work with his back to you; he seems to be multitasking between a couple different things while occasionally checking an open book sitting on the counter. Soon he notices you, his smile beaming like a ray from the sun.

"I hope you're hungry."

The End

IT WAS A GENTLE REJECTION

"Oh," is the only response you receive from Andrew. His gaze falls to his feet, along with his expression and his heart. You continue walking and Andrew seems to grow the distance between you two. Perhaps it's payback for rejecting him. His expression doesn't change at all, maybe because instead of trying to untangle several emotions, he simply simmers in a couple.

When you reach your home, Andrew takes one last look at you. He says nothing, just makes his show of disappointment very clear. It's not like he's blaming you; it's a feeling of regret.

He walks away, never to see you again.

The End

IT WAS NOT A REJECTION

Although he is definitely happy with your answer, it still seems like there's a thought floating around his head that stops him from being completely joyous. He has his eyes on you, but his expression makes it seem like he is looking through you, like his eyes are focused, but not his mind.

"Do you think …" Andrew mumbles, a thought slipping out of his mouth that spurs him into explaining, "… that I might not be able to date someone right now?"

"I have all this filming I need to do, and I'm starting up my restaurant too." Andrew's worried expression helps warm you from the cold wind picking up. "I'm afraid of making you feel neglected, I know how painful it can be." For a moment Andrew begins to mentally wander but soon he snaps back to you. "But even if I am not able see you as much as we both might want—and if it's alright with you—I'd love to try."

The End

JUST SEX

This is what you came here for, so you plan to enjoy your one night to the utmost.

You allow his hands to move freely, and freely they roam. He seems to be everywhere all at once, at one moment running his hand up between your legs, the next he's kneading both your breasts. Even as you move from the limo to his home, his hands are all over you, unwilling to become separated from your body. Your clothing, however, he is very willing to remove.

Your shoes are almost left in the car, your lust-filled mind thankfully conscious enough to grab them as you transfer to his home. The rest of your clothing is sprinkled from the front door to the bedroom.

You try to get a decent look at the house—if for nothing else than to see where you are going—but he doesn't give you the space to do so.

It's almost impressive the way Andrew unlocks his front door without removing his lips from your neck. He swings it open and slams it shut behind you two as he leads you inside.

For a moment you can hear the ringing of a phone coming from outside the bubble of lust you've created, but he doesn't give you enough room or breath to consider it. He himself seems uninterested in the phone call, all his attention focused on you.

You take a hard left and through a door, arriving in a bedroom, or so you assume as you are practically shoved atop a bed. He strips in what seems like record time before crawling over you. He doesn't waste a second, which, though rather exhilarating, makes it almost seem like he's just trying to rush through it. There's no meaningful words exchanged, no real tenderness, just a flurry of hot grasping limbs that desperately grab and claw at any patch of skin they can get to.

All too soon, like the speedy build up before it, it ends. You both collapse onto the now-damp sheets, feeling satisfied yet far more drained than you have ever felt with another person. Andrew lies beside you, not holding you, trying to bring his heaving breaths down to a normal level.

It's rather late into the night by this time, and with how physically exhausted you are now, your eyes eventually slide closed. As your consciousness begins to wander from your body, you barely hear the sound of Andrew getting dressed and leaving the room.

When you wake up a fair while later, it's not of your own volition, but by a person coming into the room. At first you gently float into a form of consciousness when you hear the opening of the bedroom door, but then you see a figure standing over you, and your fight or flight instincts slam your brain awake. In shock, and slight pain at the sudden awakening, your body jolts up into a sitting position and you scurry to the opposite side of the bed.

"Calm down," the person orders.

After your drowsy eyes focus, you realize it's a man. He looks to be in his late thirties, with strips of his light brown hair already turning grey. He wears simple sweatpants and a white t-shirt, along with an expression of utmost annoyance, it's as if you had purposely soured his day with your presence. At the very least he has the decency to look directly into your eyes rather than at your naked body.

"It's time for you to leave," he orders, throwing you your clothing that, surprisingly, has a newly-washed scent to them. "There's a washroom there, you can take a shower if you want," he says. He gestures towards a door you hadn't noticed in your blind rush of passion last night.

It's all so sudden that it takes you a moment to process what's happening. The man, obviously used to this, begins to grab the many pillows atop the bed and slip off their covers. He seems ready to wash all the sheets on the bed, unaffected by you being there.

Where's Andrew? Why isn't he here asking his guest to leave rather than this rude man shoving you out of the bed, uncaring whether you've had a decent night's sleep or not.

Then again, considering how calm this man is acting, it appears as though this might be a pattern for him. Andrew had proven the rumours of his womanizing ways true, and this was just the system that had unfolded through his many one-night stands. Perhaps you should just leave as the man has asked you to do.

Or perhaps this rude awakening has made you want to speak to Andrew even more.

Demand To See Him ➡ **PAGE 54**
Agree To Leave ➡ **PAGE 15**

LEAVE AS ASKED

Though it was said rather rudely, you accept that this is how your night with Andrew Smyth is to end.

"You want me to call you a cab or something?" the man asks as you attempt to leave. He abandons stripping the bed and walks out of the room first, making his way across the small hall to a phone sitting on a desk. "Don't worry about the fee, the cab company knows to put it on Andrew's tab."

The End

LEAVE AS ORDERED

It seems like Andrew won't be coming for you, and chasing him down would probably put him off you even more. The man now stripping the bed made it clear that you are supposed to leave.

With heavy shoulders, you turn and begin walking towards the front door, but stop in front of the writing desk. Your eyes fall upon the notepad and an idea springs into your head.

You're unable to speak to Andrew at the moment, but what if you left a trail for him to follow, if he wished? You wouldn't be forcing yourself on him, but if you wrote down your phone number he would have the option, and you could hold on to a flake of hope.

Is that going too far? It would make you look desperate in a way, and what is the likelihood that Andrew wouldn't simply throw away your number? Considering his reputation, considering how many women have tried to get more out of him, it might just be a nuisance.

Leave Phone Number ➡ PAGE 118
Do Not Leave Phone Number ➡ PAGE 55

LEAVE PHONE NUMBER

After a quick glance toward the bedroom door to make sure the grumpy man isn't going to emerge and criticize you, you grab a writing utensil. You quickly jot down your phone number before darting out, your thudding heartbeat making your adrenaline demand you escape like a fearful animal. You try to force it to slow as you take your long walk home, but once you found yourself a couple blocks away, realization strikes you.

In your haste, you had forgotten to write your name along with your phone number. How odd that would be, to find a random phone number written by your front door? Along with the question of whether Andrew would call a number he didn't recognize, you start to consider other factors, such as how long it would take him to stumble across your note.

Despite this concern, there's nothing you can do about it now. You have to wait and see if Andrew takes the bait.

You try not to concern yourself with thoughts of him, though it does pop into your mind now and again. They eventually stop a few days later when you answer the phone and, instead of a greeting, you hear your name.

"Is that you? It's Andrew."

The End

LEAVE RIGHT AFTER SEX

You decide to drag yourself out of bed, Andrew's disinterest and seeming regret at having brought you here knock at the back of your mind. After utilizing the small bathroom to clean yourself, you get dressed and leave the room.

You find Andrew standing outside the door, but not for you. He's hunched over the long desk by the door, speaking to someone on the phone as he scribbles down things on a nearby notepad. He spots you as you approach the front door, his attention snapping sharply to you.

"One second, buddy," Andrew lifts the phone away from his ear, places a hand over the microphone at the bottom. "Hey." He's speaking to you now, the first words offered in quite a while.

What could he have to say after all the time he tried to ignore you while touching you?

"Do you want to me to call you a cab?"

The End

LEAVE THE RESTAURANT

Frankly you should feel insulted, but you don't say a word. You slide out of your seat, which is quickly filled by a couple girls. You try causing as little disturbance as you can, but that doesn't stop Andrew from calling your name.

"Where are you going?" he asks. He looks away momentarily when another book to sign is shoved in his hand.

You could lie, tell him you're just going to the bathroom. Then again, do you want to give him the idea that you're coming back? That seems more cruel than telling him a form of the truth.

You tell him you're going home and don't give him much of a reason why. It doesn't seem right to tell him you don't like all the attention he's giving his fans, even if your feelings of neglect are valid.

You start walking away, your steps feel heavier with each call of your name, but each assurance from the teens that, "It's OK" that you left, quicken your pace.

Despite the mixed messages, you're able to make it outside; the cold night air hits you like a smack to the legs the moment you open the door. You know the vague direction of your home and turn to walk that way. When you make it past the end of the building, you spot a sketchy-looking man squatting behind the corner, and he notices you.

His clothing, though of some fashion, is dirty from what look to be food or liquid stains. He holds a bottle in his left hand while the other holds him steady in his low position.

"Hey there, gorgeous. You all dolled up for me?" he asks as he stands with a wicked grin.

You try to pass it off as a pleasantry and keep walking.

"Where you headin', doll? I just wanna chance to talk."

You hear his footsteps begin to follow behind you, making yours quicken along with your heartbeat.

"Really? Don't be such a bitch and just talk to me."

A large hand falls atop your shoulder and jerks it back, forcing you to turn. You're able to steady yourself and look at the man, he lifts his free hand to your face. Even as you pull way, he would have held your cheek if it wasn't for another hand coming to grab the arm of the man.

"Please, leave her alone!" Andrew demands, looking dishevelled and out of breath.

The man doesn't seem to care about Andrew's polite request, but instead turns hostile.

"Fuck off!" he yells, spinning around and swinging his arm out so fast and hard that the glass bottle he was holding shatters against the side of Andrew head.

Andrew stumbles back, holding the side of his head while the other hand reaches out to grab something to hold himself up. Even though he's able to grab hold of a metal post, his legs seem to give out and he falls to his knees.

"Jesus Christ!" The man begins to back away slowly, dropping the broken half of the bottle. "I can't go back to jail, not again." He turns on his heel and bolts down the street like his life depends on it, leaving you with Andrew who attempts to stand.

You rush over to help when he calls your name, grabbing hold of his free hand and assisting him to his feet.

"Are you OK?" he asks. Despite his gentle smile, his eyes are foggy and distant and his head seems unable to stay up, let alone still. "Thank god you're not hurt."

Though the limited light makes it difficult, you can see dark liquid oozing out from between the fingers Andrew is holding to his ear. "Don't worry about me. I just need somewhere to rest."

Somewhere to rest? But his limo and the driver have gone home seeing as he wasn't paid to stay longer. Your house is nearby—you could take him there.

Then again, you have a man barely able to stand on his own, bleeding from the side of his head. Even if he says it's fine, what if it's serious? Taking him to the hospital would be safer.

Nurse Him At Your Home ❯ **PAGE 137**
Call An Ambulance ❯ **PAGE 25**

LEAVE WITHOUT ANSWERING

You can't find it in you to tell him directly, so instead you turn away. The last you see of Andrew is a puppy-like frown that your gut tells you is an act. It's not until a couple weeks later that you start to second-guess your decision.

Andrew appears on the red carpet for the release of his newest movie, and you tune in out of morbid curiosity. You watch him stroll down the red carpet, stopping every 10 feet for pictures and questions. The smile on his face looks painted on, like mandatory makeup needed to look proper. It was not that he was too downcast to enjoy the event, more like he was not awake enough to process it all.

You find out why when one reporter asks, "Mr. Smyth, many people have noticed that you have been leaving parties alone lately. And so we have to ask, for all those hopeful girls out there: Have you finally found yourself a special lady?"

Andrew's chuckle is dry, not filled with humour, but a feeble attempt to cover up the pain of a bad memory.

"I thought I did, she just didn't feel the same way."

The End

LET HIM BE WOKEN UP

You watch Zach leave back up the stairs, and once again you're left by yourself, but it doesn't feel quite as lonely as before thanks to the knowledge that you'll be joined soon.

Nevertheless, you have nothing to do for a time, so your eyes inevitably wander back to the pictures. You study them a little closer, finding yourself becoming a bit of a detective. You look through each picture, trying to deduce who the fading man is.

It doesn't take long for you to connect the puzzle pieces. You deduce who Andrew's mother is based on a picture of a young Andrew and two other young girls holding up Mother's Day cards while standing around a woman. Next you notice that the man is in pictures with that same woman in photos where she looks younger than the ones with Andrew. Finally, there's a set of pictures of Andrew's mom in the hospital holding a newborn baby. There are three. One is of the man and a single child wrapped in a pink blanket snuggled close to the woman. The next is of the woman lying in bed with another tightly bundled baby in a pink blanket, a young girl curled up beside the woman looking down at the bundle, the man sitting beside them. Finally, there's a picture of the woman in a hospital bed once again, this time holding a bundle of blue with both previous girls huddled at her side, but no man.

You look at one last picture, one of what looks to be Andrew at kindergarten age. He stands sandwiched between his sisters, all putting on what look to be fake smiles as the man from before stands behind them, looking worse for wear.

"Crack head," Andrew mumbles, reaching a hand past you so he can slide the picture and its frame down flat, hiding it from view. His face is nothing short of a scowl, but he shakes it off fast once he notices you looking. "Sorry, just some personal feelings. Anyway, I'm so glad you're still here." Andrew's smile is bright, and so far from what you had just witnessed, like the last few seconds didn't happen.

"I wanted to talk to you, about how much we talked, actually," he says. He starts to walk away from the shelf of pictures, as if leading you away from them. "I know this may sound odd, but I don't actually talk to that many girls, at least not the way you and I have."

Andrew pulls out a chair from the large dining table, but instead of sitting down in it, he twirls it around and offers it to you.

"Whenever women talk to me lately, it's either co-workers that are bored, or women who are purely doing it with an end goal in mind, but I don't get that feeling with you." He grabs a seat for himself this time and turns it to face you directly. "Not that I'm trying to persuade you off of having any sort of feelings for me, but I simply can't explain how much I've enjoyed this wonderfully peaceful conversation we've had." He sits down, hands folding on his lap as he gets comfortable in the seat like he expects to be there for quite some time. "No ulterior motives, no forced pleasantries, just two people speaking on equal terms. I hoped we could continue on like that. I have nothing else to do for today, and to be honest, I've spoken so much about myself and my dreams for the future …"

Andrew's smile is calm while his eyes very focused, like you had suddenly become the most interesting thing in the world. "I would love to hear more about you."

The End

LET HIM ESCORT YOU

Andrew's expression lights up when you agree; he practically jumps from his seat, newfound energy burning in him. He holds out a hand to you and you take it as your numb legs have a bit of trouble holding you up. As feeling comes back to your lower half, you look over at your friend who gives you a gentle smile and nod.

"I'll call you later then. Have a good night, you two," she says just as you find the strength to stand on your own and pull your hand away from Andrew's. Despite her goodbye, you three end up following each other out.

In an attempt to avoid awkwardness, she takes this as an opportunity to give a joking shovel talk.

"Now don't you keep her out too late. And if I find out you made her cry, I'm gonna make you cry." She's slightly intoxicated and it seems to be urging her to a more relaxed state than she would usually allow anyone other than friends to see.

"You don't have to worry," Andrew responds. The look he gives you while saying this is intense in its sincerity, so much so that your friend notices and giggles for you.

"Don't go getting married now," she teases, scampering away and laughing to herself louder then she probably realizes.

Once she disappears into the limo you had arrived in, Andrew offers you his elbow, hoping to link arms with you. You begin your walk home and, though he is able to distract you for a while with conversation, eventually the wind nipping at your skin brings on so much discomfort that he notices. Instinctively you curl into yourself a bit, crossing your arms in hopes of gaining a bit of warmth.

"Are you alright? I would offer you my jacket if I had one."

His waistcoat wouldn't really help you, so instead he raises his arm. He starts to stretch it around your back before stopping.

"May I?" he asks you, but his eyes are directed at his own arm, the brief moment where your gazes connect is enough to pinken his cheeks. "Excuse me," he whispers as he carefully wraps his shaky arm around your shoulders. "There, a bit better?"

You can feel warmth radiating from Andrew, even more so when he gains enough courage to pull you a little closer. His lips quiver, as if he's fighting down the urge to smile more then he already was. After a long moment of embarrassed silence, the conversation starts up again. In time, Andrew becomes more relaxed, regaining the same attentive and friendly conversation as before, though his flirty comments become harder for him to make as his eyes feel the need to dart away every time.

Eventually you reach your home, forcing Andrew to slide his arms off your shoulders. You open the door, and you can see by the way he glances at you that he has something to say, it just takes him a minute to work up the courage.

"Look," he starts, hands coming together so they could play. "I'm not sure what you did to me but … I haven't felt this stupidly giddy in so long. Let alone with a woman." His eyes meet yours and his grin only widens, his pink cheeks get a little brighter. "I know this may seem like some sort of puppy love, perhaps it is, but I want to see where this might go, you and me." Andrew stumbles over a few more sentences but his hope is clear.

A bashful request to be the girlfriend of one of the most popular actors in the country? A womanizer who doesn't know what to do with himself when he's stricken with emotional attraction rather then physical? It sounds adorable, but does it sound a little too sudden? "Puppy love" he called it, would it last? Was this like a one-night stand, a short emotional affectation?

Or perhaps there are sincere feelings behind his blushing cheeks. This is for you to decide.

Will you risk it?

Risk Puppy Love ➲ **PAGE 143**
Don't Risk Puppy Love ➲ **PAGE 68**

LET HIM SIT WITH YOU

"No, go ahead." You accept as you turn to look up at the man and your mouth falls open. It—it was him, there's no mistaking it. You've seen him several times, though there was always a screen separating you two. It was Andrew Smyth.

A grin spreads across his face at your reaction before he places a single finger atop his lips.

"Shhh, no one else knows I'm here yet, and I'd like to keep it that way," he says as he takes the open seat beside you. He orders himself a drink, an Adam's Ale, and you take the opportunity to look him over.

His inky black hair is casually hanging down free, his bangs covering just the top of his eyes. The back strands of hair are cut in a way that make a distinct V-shape on the back of his neck, yet long enough on top to get a good grip on, if the situation did arrive.

His eyebrows are softly peaked and almost unnoticeably lighter than the hair atop his head. He has upturned eyes that, though not as bright as some candid pictures, are a forest green shining ever so slightly, as if they have dim lights behind them.

His chin is pointed with a bit of a bump sitting under a shadow created by his out turned lips, making them an alluring target.

He is wearing an obviously-tailored, dark grey waistcoat with an ashy, light blue shirt; the combination makes his upper body look larger than usual. He's wearing only one simple accessory: a navy blue tie with some silver threads subtly laced in.

You had seen him through a screen and on paper many times, but having him sit there in front of you doesn't feel quite real, yet here he was. He is so close, you could reach out and touch him.

"Something the matter, miss?" he asks, a knowing smile on his lips. You can't form an answer, however, before the humour in his eyes dies down and he shifts in his seat to face you better. "What's your story, if you're willing to tell it? New to the high society scene or just too shy to show up to the parties? Because I don't recall ever seeing you around before, and I would definitely remember a face like yours." He speaks with the utmost confidence, as if hitting on a woman was as simple a task as opening a door.

It takes you a moment to collect your thoughts before you explain your situation, which proves to be a bit challenging what with the way he takes the time to look at each of your eyes, studying them with an intensity that almost forces you to do the same.

"I see," he says before sipping away the last of his drink. "If I may say: I do see the flaws in your friend's tactics, but it sounds like her heart is in the right place. And I do agree with her." He turns in his seat to face you with his whole body. "Your participation tonight has already blessed one lucky man, what do you say to giving him a chance to show the rest of the guests what a bewitching beauty is on the dance floor?" He holds out his hand in a sudden offering.

A dance with a handsome, rich man? It sounds like the dream every man-loving person wants at one point or another. Or is it too good to be true?

You could go out there with him and live the dream for a couple minutes, but do you really want all these high-class people watching you—nameless you—with judging eyes?

Then again, when are you ever going to get the chance to dance with Andrew Smyth again? When does anyone get the chance to dance with a celebrity, unless they're a star as well? His hand will be in yours, your bodies will be pressed together, your faces so close …

Dance ➲ PAGE 48
Decline Dance ➲ PAGE 136

LET HIM SLEEP AND LEAVE

The out-of-touch feeling weighs heavy on you, to the point where you'd rather leave. Besides, it would be rude to wake someone up just because you're bored. When you declare that you wish to go home, Zach freezes mid-step and looks to you.

"Really? Andrew's just upstairs, I could go get him real easy." It's an offer that he seems more interested in doing than you.

Nevertheless you stand your ground and again request to be let free to go home.

"Oh, well …" Zach looks up the staircase for a moment, the questioning in his mind evident in his expression. "How about I call you a cab?" he offers which, considering the sun is currently setting, you decide to take.

Zach leads you upstairs and slowly meanders to the phone beside the front door and calls you a ride. Before you can decide whether you want to wait outside or not, Zach quickly strikes up a conversation. It's supposed to be just light chitter-chatter but his eyes keep glancing past you to the staircase, his words stumble and occasionally he needs you to repeat things. He even goes so far as to claim that you've forgotten something but you know you haven't.

You leave the home with a stammering Zach seeing you off.

By the time you're pulling out of the driveway, the front door is closed, not that it really matters anymore. The cab driver you have is the quiet type, content in simply asking you where you want to be taken and leaving it at that. Because of this, and the traffic you're quickly caught up in, you're left to sit alone in the backseat with just your thoughts—thoughts that inevitably drift to Andrew.

They're eventually interrupted when you hear someone calling your name.

Suddenly the world begins blaring with noise, a few car honks, a couple of people yell things, and the distinct voice of Andrew calls to you. You try sticking your head out the window to see if Andrew really is somewhere nearby, but it doesn't work with your position and so you're forced to step out of the vehicle.

You rise to a standing position and your name is called again, this time less like a question and more like an excited realization. You see that Andrew is, in fact, running down the street between cars towards you. He's limping slightly, thanks to his bare feet and the road being rough to run on.

When he reaches you he tries to talk immediately but is interrupted by heavy breaths. His chest is bare and all he's wearing is a pair of sweatpants, but the cold evening air doesn't seem to affect him enough to move his attention away from you.

"Why did you leave?" He is able to say between his intakes of air. "Did I do something wrong?"

Andrew waits for your response, but it seems no one else is willing to do as such because the drivers all around you start to get agitated.

"Get out of the way!"

"The hell you think you doin'?"

People are yelling out their windows and honking, pressuring you to react in some way. On the far left and right you can see some pedestrians looking your way, a couple of them stop, some even pull out their phones.

"We can't stay here, come back to my place." Andrew holds his hand out to you.

"Move it!" someone says.

Should you go with him? He seems so desperate to talk to you, so much so that he is not only embarrassing himself, but also physically hurting himself by running out here without getting prepared. All this just so he could catch you before you could leave.

"Some of use have places to be!" yells another driver.

But this is kind of ridiculous, isn't it? You can't ditch a cab because the person you just left decides they didn't want you to leave yet. Besides, do you really want to go back to a place you feel lost in?

"You're not the only people in the world!"

You need to make a decision, now.

Take His Hand And Go Back ⮕ **PAGE 162**
Get Back In The Car ⮕ **PAGE 77**

MAKE ENOUGH FOR JUST YOU

At the very least, you need food. You could pay Andrew back for whatever you use later, but right now your stomach is starting to hurt you in protest at not being filled.

You make your way downstairs, through the dining room, and into the huge kitchen. It's a bit overbearing; there's multiple sets of ovens, sinks and utensils. You make your way to the three doors on the left side of the room that make up a walk-in cupboard, fridge and freezer. Despite their large size, they're not completely packed as the kitchen behind you would imply. It's stocked like someone preparing for a house party, which may very well be true considering Andrew did mention he cooked for his whole family weekly.

You don't spend too long in the kitchen. You make yourself the most minimalist breakfast you can come up with. Every dish you dirty, you clean, and everything you touch you return to its place. You make it look as if you had never been here; in a sense it feels as if you weren't.

As you sat there, eating your basic breakfast, you feel an unnerving sense of abnormality, like you're out of place, like you shouldn't be there. You're surrounded by someone else's money, and another family's memories. You're the odd one out, knowing nothing about the circumstances of these pictures and awards, aside from what you've been told the past 24 hours. You're not barging in, but you also don't belong.

You try to distract yourself from these thoughts by gazing at the pictures around the room. Though it doesn't help to clear your head all that much, it does bring something rather interesting to your attention. As you look through the photos, mentally placing them in chronological order, you notice a pattern. Over time, while Andrew ages, it seems one man fades away. The man starts by appearing in many pictures, but fewer and fewer are taken with him in it until he just stops appearing at all.

"You're still here?"

Your head snaps up, mind whipping from its wandering thoughts to Zach standing at the bottom of the stairs carrying a bucket of dirty water.

"So, Andrew's not up yet, huh? What a guy, to leave a lady waiting. I'm gonna go get him, you just hold tight a little longer."

Zach places the bucket down and prepares to head to Andrew's room, wherever that may be, but something inside of your brain, urges you to stop him.

You've been soaking in your feelings of alienation, and there's a subtle growing desire to go home, back to a place you don't feel like you're intruding on. This is your chance to go home, and you could always leave your phone numbers with Zach so Andrew could contact you later if he wishes.

But to wake up to find your guest having walked out on you—that would be awfully hurtful. At the very least you should stick around long enough to thank Andrew.

Let Him Be Woken Up ➡ PAGE 124
Let Him Sleep And Leave ➡ PAGE 131

DECLINE DANCE

Even though the offer is enticing, you shake your head lightly. You can't do it, risk embarrassing yourself in front of all these high society people, let alone Andrew Smyth.

"I can't really dance," you say, the truth in this statement is variable. You see his expression fall slightly as he freezes both mentally and physically for a moment. He had been so confident that you would agree that your rejection has thrown him off kilter. Soon though he jumps back on the horse to try again.

"That's alright. If I'm being honest, I'm not the best dancer either, but what does that matter when we are enjoying ourselves?" He offers his hand again, reaching out for yours, but you pull away, insisting that you stay off the dance floor. You see disappointed defeat in his eyes as he pulls back his hand, but before you can start feeling too bad for him, he switches his tactics.

"That's fine. How about we just talk a bit over a drink then? Whatever you want, on me."

He is being rather persistent, which some could see as a compliment, yet others may find it unsettling. How do you see it?

Drink ➡ PAGE 69
Decline Drink ➡ PAGE 51

NURSE HIM AT YOUR HOME

He asked you for a simple place to rest, forcing him into an ambulance may frighten his confused mind.

Not being sure how well a taxi driver will take a bloody man getting into his cab, you decide to walk the few blocks to your home. It takes a bit to get him going, but once you pass the first block, Andrew stops dragging his feet. By the time you're on your street, he can stand on his own, though he still holds onto you, wrapping himself around your one arm like a very affectionate girlfriend.

"Thank you," he mumbles as you let him into your house. "May I use the washroom to clean myself?"

You give him your blessing and he stumbles his way to the bathroom. You follow behind, an innate need to help the bleeding man moving you forward, but you're stopped at the door.

"I'm sorry, but I would like to do this myself. I've bothered you enough tonight, I don't want to subject you to having to clean this idiotic head of mine." His smile hides shame that he knew could be seen, but he would not speak of it.

He closes the door carefully, leaving you to wait in your home, listening to the flow of water and occasional grunts of pain. The only form of update you receive is when Andrew asks to borrow a pair of tweezers, for what he doesn't say.

As the minutes tick on, the physical and emotional strain grows heavier, especially on your eyelids. You try to stay awake, not wanting to, in a sense, abandon Andrew in his predicament. However, once you got into a comfortable enough position, your mind gives way.

You wake up to an afternoon sun and someone banging at your door. Despite the incisive knocking, you take a moment to absorb your surroundings. Most things seem to be as you left them, but there are a couple differences. Atop you now lies your blanket, one you don't recall having grabbed. On the coffee table there's a decent-sized, handwritten, note on plain, lined paper. Finally, there's a million-dollar actor curled up snug on a chair, sleeping.

Andrew is still wearing his pants, but had removed his waistcoat. He's only in a blue undershirt that now has a faint red stain on one side of the collar. Socks still on, he had removed his shoes, which are sitting neatly side by side on the floor. His position looks rather uncomfortable, his hip lies sideways on the seat and he had forced his large body to curl up enough for him to rest is head on the arm of the chair, hiding the spot where the wound was. It was enough for him though as he is fast asleep.

The knock at the door begins knocking at your brain, dragging you to your feet. On the way up you grab the note, reading it as you slowly made your way to your door.

> *Good morning, I hope you slept well.*
>
> *As you may have noticed, I am still here. I had planned to—*

Your foot catches on something, making a sharp noise escape your throat as you stumble forward. You are able to regain your footing before hitting the ground and, after a moment to breathe, you continue forward.

> *I had planned to leave once I finished cleaning up but realized that I have no way to lock the door behind me.*
>
> *Because of this, I hope you don't mind that I stayed the night. I felt leaving the door open was putting you at risk,*

You reach your front door, unlocking it without looking up from the note.

Especially from the scummier men and women who think it's worth breaking into someone's home for a scoop.

Scoop?

You open up the door and are blinded by rapid-fire flashes of lights. You cover your eyes instinctually, hearing a flurry of voices as your vision adjusts. Eventually you're able to see, your arm still held up to block the lights like a visor, and find microphones shoving past one another to be closer to you.

"Where is Andrew Smyth now? Is he alright?"

"Who are you?"

"Why didn't you take Andrew to the hospital after the attack?"

"Did you know that the attacker almost got away because of your negligence?"

"What do you say to the allegations that this is an attempted kidnapping?"

"The media seems to have had a busy morning." This voice was gentler, kind, and came from behind you.

Andrew is standing to your left, one of his hands on your right shoulder. Though he looks like he's just been jarred from his short sleep, his actor smile was shining over it.

Now you can see the side of his head where he had been struck, but instead of a scar or blood, his hair is clean. If you hadn't seen it with your own eyes, you wouldn't have known he was injured. Perhaps the amount of blood that had come from his head was a misjudgement of the actual severity of the cuts.

While you study the side of his head, the paparazzi continue to ask questions, now aimed towards the star.

"Please, everyone. One question at a time," Andrew says. He squeezes your shoulder ever so slightly and looks down at you with the same smile painted on his lips, but his eyes shift to ones of concern.

"What really happened this morning?" asks a reporter, knowing how to get all her answers in the fewest words possible.

"Well," Andrew turns from you to the woman asking the question, "after insinuating something rather rude, I was lucky enough to go on a date with this lovely lady here." Andrew lifts his free hand to motion towards you. "Unfortunately, I made an idiotic mistake, after which I attempted to be a Prince Charming but ended up making a fool of myself. However, she was kind enough to give me a place to rest. I just hope she's willing to give me a fourth chance—not that I really deserve it after all I put her through."

The End

POLITELY DECLINE

You pull your leg away from him and give a gentle smile. You tell him that you appreciate the offer, but you're not interested. His mouth practically falls open at your words but you don't give him any time to pick his jaw up off the floor. You turn to the bartender and ask if he can call you a cab.

"Wait, a cab, where are you going?" Andrew asks, not that it's really any of his business. It's clear, however, that he's confused rather than having bad intentions.

You inform him that you're simply going home and wish him a good night. You stand, leaving him to sit there and watch you go. It's a bittersweet moment, walking away from a man that has defied his friendly-seeming persona by treating you the way he did, but you keep your chin up.

You find your friend and explain that you're uncomfortable and wish to go home. After a little questioning, she apologizes for not only having to stay but forcing you to come in the first place. She gives you a hug and sends you on your way.

You return to the bar so you can ask the gentleman behind the counter which company he called and where they would be parked. Despite purposely walking to the opposite end of the bar, you take the time to see if Andrew is still sitting where you left him. In fact, he's not, possibly off looking for a new candidate to take home with him.

You walk outside and are practically unnoticed by the paparazzi but, oddly enough, you get a shy glance from Andrew Smyth as he passes by you. It's an awkward exchange but you keep it polite as he goes in the opposite direction, back into the party.

You make your way down a couple blocks, away from the many limos and posh cars parked outside, until you spot your ride home.

The trip is uneventful to say the least, the driver makes no attempt at chatting you up. Your house is not that far from where the party was taking place so you are, thankfully, there in no time.

You ask about the bill as you reach for some money, but the driver stops you.

"Already paid for, ma'am," he says plainly, waving off your attempt. "Oh, and that reminds me," he adds, "I was asked to give you this." He reaches down into the glove compartment and pulls out a napkin-sized piece of paper. You accept it and try to give a thank you but are interrupted by his phone ringing. Politely, you hurry out of the cab and it pulls away immediately.

You stand there awkwardly for a moment before looking down at the slip of paper. It looks like there was once a paragraph on it, and you can make out bits here and there like "*making you uncomfortable*" and "*went too far,*" but most is covered up by a hasty scribble from the non-erasable pen used to write it. All that is fully visible is a simple "*Sorry,*" signed Andrew Smyth.

The End

RISK PUPPY LOVE

You accept, and for a moment, Andrew looks puzzled, as if thrown off by your assuring smile, but then a grin breaks through.

"Really?" he asks, to which you repeat your answer.

"Th—thank you. May I have your number?" He begins to fumble slightly, with his words and hands as he pulls out his phone. By the way he grumbles each time he slips up, it's obvious he's frustrated in himself. "Sorry, I'm a bit nervous."

Just like before, he can't seem to bring his eyes up to look at you. "I haven't had a night end like this in many years." His shoulders stiffen, his eyes open wide in shocked realization. He decides not to verbally show his regret, instead focusing on swapping phone numbers.

"Alright, so I'll call you later then," he says, signalling what should be a cue to leave. Instead he stands there, watching you with a nervous grin before taking a step closer to you and holding out his arms. Andrew waits for you to reject, and when you don't, he wraps his arms around your waist. He pulls you into an embrace and, for a moment, just holds you in his arms, as if savouring the feeling. The warmth coming off of him is comforting, gentle and innocent. Then, without warning, he pulls back just enough so he can press his lips to your cheek.

"Sweet dreams," he whispers as he pulls away. "I definitely will."

He strolls backwards, eyes glued to you like he can't get enough of you. His smile shines with the giddiness of a man who has successfully completed their first date, and, once he believes he's out of sight, you catch him break into an excited skip.

The End

SAVE HIM

You decide to play along, watching Mr. Finster's expression fall as Andrew's smile tries not to break into a humorous one.

"So, if you'll excuse us," Andrew says, his grin becoming smug as he leads you back to the bar where you met.

"Have you ever considered becoming an actor?" Andrew asks as he waits for you to take your seat before gracefully sliding onto his stool. "Thanks for the help. It seems like I can never escape people offering me positions." For a moment his suave expression cracks into one of annoyance and fatigue, but it doesn't show for long. "So, what do you want to drink?"

The night continues with you two chatting about a surprising array of various things; you slowly move about the room, with an occasional dance thrown in. Along with that, throughout the party people approach Andrew: some offering business propositions, others asking questions like they might be undercover reporters, and many women who flaunt themselves in front of him. Some even have the nerve to try and wrap their arms around him, but Andrew promptly shoos them away after a quick greeting.

"I'm doing well with my date here, thank you," is his usual answer, his hand making contact with you, whether on your shoulder, around your waist, or other places. "So, if you'll excuse us," he says with a stern smile showing that he was not in the mood for negotiations. Whether you two took the leave or the interrupters did, his hand always held you for a bit longer than necessary.

Along with that, in between the interruptions, when you could speak in peace, the conversations had flirtatious tones sprinkled in most everywhere. He wasn't particularly subtle about it, smooth sure, but not hidden at all. It was blatant, spoken like they were facts, not caring whether the others around you overheard or not.

You end up spending the remainder of the party with him, until your friend approaches and informs you that it's about time you and her head home—though she's unable to suppress a squeal of excitement at whom you had spent your night with.

"Is it that time already?" Andrew questions as he looks up at a distant clock. "Well, would you look at that, guess we lost track of time," he says as he turns to you with the smile that has been stuck to his face most of the night. By now it has shifted to be a bit friendlier than his original purely flirtatious one.

"Have a good night, Mr. Smyth," your friend says dramatically, like she wants to show off to anyone else still at the party, not realizing that most of them have been watching you anyway.

You also say your goodbye but as you begin to turn and walk away, Andrew grabs your hand and pulls you back to him. The sudden force causes you to stumble, leading you to cling to his shoulders to steady yourself.

"Or, you could come with me," he whispers in your ear, freezing you in place. "The party may be over, but the night is still young, so how about it?"

Will you go with him? Continue this wonderful night with this handsome man?

Or would you rather keep the night sweet and innocent by taking your leave? This was fun, and maybe you can get his number so you can keep in contact.

Don't Go Home With Him ❯ PAGE 56
Go To His Home ❯ PAGE 93

SAY YOU WANT MORE

You can't accept this—just being brushed off as another woman that has shared Andrew's bed. You want more, more of the fun times you had at the party, more time with him. When you tell him this he looks put off, like your desire for a relationship is out of nowhere. You see him glance at the man stuffing the sheets into the opal red hamper, as if silently asking for input.

"It's up to you, man," the man says. "But I will remind you that you've had a couple chicks do this. How have those turned out?"

Andrew tsks and looks down at the floor, losing himself in thought. The other man leaves the room, giving the actor's shoulders a pat.

"Good luck, man."

"Thanks, Zach." Andrew throws over his shoulder as the man disappears from sight.

For a moment Andrew ponders, eyes looking up at you every time you speak to show that he's being attentive to what you're saying. Eventually he decides on what to do next, again leaving you to his whim. "I will say that I had fun talking with you last night, so I'll take your number. That's about all I can offer right now, I'm still tired from working. Is that alright?"

It wasn't like you had any other option, so you follow Andrew out of the room and to a desk sitting across the hall. There's a notepad on it, along with the phone you heard last night. You write down your name and number and hand it over to Andrew who's busy covering an escaping yawn. That paired with the light crescents under his eyes make his exhaustion obvious.

How long had he stayed up to work? What was he working on?

You don't get to ask as he kindly guides you out the door. Maybe you can ask him, if he ever calls.

The End

SHAKE HANDS AND MAKE PLANS

You take his hand and give it a shake, which blows away his shy fear. The grip he offers back is strong, like he's not quite sure things are real but doesn't want to let go just in case you might fade away if he does.

Unfortunately, he is forced to release you when your car starts to drift from his. The limo you're riding in is making a right turn, something Andrew's driver could not predict despite being ordered to follow your vehicle. As you're forced further and further apart, Andrew leans more out of the window so he can keep hold of your hand, but eventually he has to let go or one of you might get injured. You can see him watch you intently and just barely hear him yell something out to you but you can't make it out, and, eventually, he disappears behind the corner of a building.

There's a long pause as both you and your friend stare out the window, as if waiting for Andrew to just appear again, but of course he doesn't. Finally your friend begins to speak, it takes her a couple of sentences to pull your eyes away from the window. She tries to reassure you, commenting on how there can't be that many limos driving around this early in the morning, even with the party having just ended, but you can tell that she, herself, has doubts.

Andrew never catches up with your car, leaving you to accept that fate and go home. He doesn't leave your thoughts, however, no matter how much you may want him to. Even if it does bring on negative feelings, it drives you to attempt to get in contact with him.

You could try and call out to him on social media, but with hundreds of thousands of people messaging him everyday, how likely was he to see you? You could try finding out where he works or who his agent is, but those are all kept so secretive, thanks to intense fans. You could try going to another event he might attend, but those only happen every few months, and by then he might have lost interest.

There's nothing you can do, at least not alone. Your friend attempts to help by tracking down Andrew Smyth's agent, that being as far she can get with her small star power. You do call his agent and explain your situation, but you're met with a woman that curtly informs you that she was far to busy to pass along messages to Mr. Smyth from a woman that he had apparently "met and agreed to hang out with." Just by the way the woman says it, it sounds like you're not the first person to call and claim to know Andrew.

So, after giving your number, which will most likely be tossed before Andrew gets even a glimpse of it, you hang up.

One day, not too long after your phone conversation, you're home alone when someone knocks on your door. You casually waltz over to open it up and find a bouquet—so large the plastic wrapping around the stems is almost flat like a disc.

"Good afternoon," Andrew greets you, moving the bouquet to his side so you can see his full form. His hair, though a bit tousled by what seems to be nervous fingers run through them, is freshly washed. The clothing he wears is pressed, pristine white button-up shirt and black dress pants.

"I'm so glad it's actually you," he says smiling. He looks relieved, like a hot air balloon worth of stress has just blown away. "I was a bit worried that your friend may have misled me. Oh, and I must apologize for how rude my agent was to you, and for not actually taking down your number." Andrew's shoulders tense as his smile grows sheepish. "I hope you're still willing to spend time with me, despite that."

The End

SHOWER WITH HIM

This romantic movie that has become your life seems to be going great, so why should the credits start rolling now?

You arise from the bed and the cold afternoon air hits your warm body like a jump into the ocean. Goosebumps prickle your skin, while other parts of your body react in their own ways. It's not long before Andrew slides to your side of the bed and stands as well, his arms slowly wrap around you as he leans close to your ear. You can feel the full front side of his body as he presses up against you, Andrew wanting as much contact as possible.

"It's alright, I'll keep you warm."

And he leads you into the bathroom to do just that, and give you a shower as well.

The End

SLAP HIM

The crisp sound rings out as your hand collides with his cheek, the room is hushed to silence immediately. Andrew looks at you with shock, his eyes filled with something that could be hurt, as the rest of the room's attention moves to you two.

"You conceited jackass!" you shout as you stand from your seat. He thinks he can call you "pretty" and you'll just fall into his bed?

Before his scrambled brain can even come up with a retort, you turn on your heels and walk away, determined to find your friend and demand to be taken home.

How dare he, how dare anyone think they can talk to a person for a mere couple minutes before offering sex? In this moment, chivalry feels truly dead.

You storm your way through the crowd and find your friend who, thankfully, doesn't ask a thing at the moment. She had heard the slap and now that she sees your expression, she puts two and two together. She grabs your hand and leads you out of the building, pushing through the paparazzi with ease, and pulling you into one of the awaiting limos.

You ride all the way to her house in boiling anger, not processing the significance of what you had done until well into your sporadic sleepover. At some point, however, the realization comes crumbling down on you. But no matter how you react to it, there's nothing to be done.

You eventually fall asleep with the hope of putting it all behind you, but wake up to find it getting shoved back in your face.

"Come on, get up, you have to see this," your friend demands as she flashes her bright phone in your face. "I think you started a revolution." Reluctantly you rise into a sitting position and take the phone.

The screen is a paused on a YouTube video of what looks like a news report or talk show. A man is sitting at a plain desk, he looks to be in his late thirties; a younger woman sits beside him. Though obviously confused and a tad worried, you accept fate and press play while your friend snuggles up beside you so she can see the screen as well.

"Next on our list is something I personally really like," starts the woman. "So, as some might know, the current Hollywood heartthrob Andrew Smyth, recently attended another of the many charity events going on this year," she says with a hand gesture to her partner who nods in agreement.

"He usually does, Hailey," says the man, seemingly unaware of what the woman was about to speak of.

"True, but he probably wishes he hadn't come to this one."

"Oh?" the older gentleman responds, resting his elbow on the desk in front of them in intrigue.

"Yes, because that night he decided he was on the prowl."

"Sounds like him," the man jokes, receiving a quick giggle from the woman.

"Why else would he go?" Hailey jokes back before returning to her original topic. "But the girl who caught his eye, who we sadly don't know the name of as she was written as a 'plus one' on the guest list, rejected his offer." The woman continues almost proudly as the man's eyebrows rise in curiosity. "But that's not the best part," she adds.

"There's more?"

"Oh, hell yes! Instead of just saying 'no,' she gave him a full on slap to the face."

The man burst out laughing as the woman also couldn't hold in her giggles.

"Really?!"

"Yeah, we have a video here," the woman says as a video of you, on loop, giving Andrew Smyth an almost movie scene perfect slap across the cheek, comes on screen. The sound is cut off, however, and replaced by the two hosts' laughter.

Eventually it fades back to the couple at the desk as they calm to light chuckles between words.

"You don't understand how much I love this," Hailey finally says.

"But don't you feel kind of bad for him?" asks the older man.

Hailey shook her head sternly in reply. "Not at all," she says with close to no hesitation.

"Isn't it a little harsh though?"

"I don't think so. I've been waiting for someone to show men that just because he's high in society and attractive doesn't mean all women are going to fall at his feet. And *you*, lady," the women says, pointing a finger at the camera. "I hope you're watching this so I can tell you how awesome you are for standing up against those over confident slime balls. You go girl!"

The End

STAND HIM UP

It simply doesn't seem real. A Cinderella night with a celebrity now asking you to come back? What's next, a marriage proposal? Perhaps your friend's warnings of Andrew being a womanizer are getting to you, or maybe it's your own doubt, either way, the risk of getting hurt is not worth the momentary fantasy.

However, there would be one thing that is most definitely horrible about this decision: the wait. The party is another month away, and even if you're not planning to go to it, it'll be like waiting for a lie to be revealed—the countdown to the night of the party will be almost painful.

Maybe you could talk to people about your situation, but what will they say, what will they think? They will most likely choose sides and possibly put pressure on you over what to do.

It wouldn't matter who you did or did not speak to though, because the night of the party suddenly arrives, despite the long, dreadful wait leading up to it.

You try to go about your evening like usual, try to ignore the temptation of looking up the event and watching a live stream. The attempt, however, is in vain, as your friend, having naturally been invited to the event herself, starts sending you text messages.

Hey

So I just had a bit of a chat with a certain celebrity that's waiting for his date.

Along with the words, she attaches a picture. It's of a very elaborate looking doorway with elaborate looking people crowded into a room beyond it. Standing beside the door, staring out and away from the building, holding a single rose in his hand, was Andrew. His stance showed that he would not be abandoning his post, despite the smile stretched across his face being one of fading hope.

I know this is kind of my fault for warning you about him, but seeing him standing there is just sad. I just thought you should know.

What was this, a guilt trip? After she told you not to go for him? And now she's texting you sad messages …

Then again, it did seem kind of sad, standing there alone outside of the party. And perhaps your friend was legitimately regretful about the things she said before.

But should that change anything? You knew something like this would happen. Besides, he did say you had the right to decline the offer.

Still Don't Go To The Party ➡ **PAGE 160**
Go To The Party After Trying To Stand Him Up ➡ **PAGE 95**

START GETTING SEXUAL

You turn in your seat so you face Andrew, giving him the same sultry gaze he's giving you. This makes his grin widen, like a sophisticated villain whose plan is playing out as expected. He makes the first move, not giving you the chance to do anything, moving quickly as if he'd been simply waiting for you to give the OK.

He leans towards you, making sure his head is higher than yours, forcing you to look up at him like you're willing prey. He bends down, letting his lips brush against yours, but doesn't let himself kiss you. He makes you rise to meet him, letting you get a quick kiss, but then slowly pulling away, leading you into chasing his lips until your sitting in his lap.

The night continues as such: Andrew stringing you along and rewarding you with more affection when you move as he silently instructs. Even when moving from the limo to his home, he has a finger hooked into the front of your bra over your clothing, leading you into the building. His eyes demand your attention, making it hard to see anything else, though you do spot a large, muscular man that holds the car door open for you two. But that's all you catch as Andrew tugs you along.

He pulls you into his home, but you don't see much of it. For a brief moment you hear a phone ringing, but Andrew insists that you ignore it. He leads you away from the bothersome noise into a room just left of the entrance, and so it begins.

All of Andrew's movements are slow and calculated, like he knows exactly what to do and how to do it. Perhaps he does, considering all the practise he's gotten in the past—something your friend had warned you about. But you don't think much of it, you can't with the way Andrew makes you play his game. He seems most comfortable when he's in control, hence why he doesn't give you the chance to be.

Even when you wake up the next morning, it seems as though he has decided the fate of your relationship by leaving you alone in the room.

You awaken to the sound of the door opening, but it's not Andrew coming to greet you. It's another man who doesn't seem surprised to see you—in fact, it seem like he's a tad annoyed by it.

"You're still here?" he asks, but doesn't wait for you to answer. Instead he walks into the room, pulling a laundry basket on wheels behind him. "I got cleaning to do, lady, so if you could hurry up and get ready to leave, that would be great."

Without giving you time to get off the bed, the man starts grabbing the scattered pillows and removing the covers on them.

You're practically being forced out of the bed, and so use the time it takes you to get dressed to think through what is happening.

Leave … the man just told you point blank to leave like he owns this place. He just barges in on you while you're still naked, and expects you to just get dressed and leave. And what about Andrew, where is he, and why is he letting this man boss you around?

If you were to look at it from their perspective, however, this may just be the pattern that has arisen from all the one-night stands Andrew has had. You know his reputation and agreed to this, so maybe this is just the outcome you have to expect.

Leave As Asked ❂ **PAGE 116**
Ask To See Him ❂ **PAGE 19**

STAY ON THE LINE

He asked you to stay, hanging up would be rude. Besides, he seems so excited to have you call him.

Even with these thoughts, it doesn't stop the detached feeling of seeing someone that's supposed to be talking to you talking to a dozen others while you sit silently on the other side of a screen.

"Is it true that you're working on a secret project?"

"Perhaps." His eyes hold a sly excitement behind them as he sticks his empty hand in his pocket.

"Could you tell us more?"

"Well then it's not a secret then is it?"

"Who are you talking to on the phone?"

"Is it about your project?"

"Is it a girl?"

"A woman, and perhaps."

Andrew briefly looks to you and gives a wink, something that the paparazzi take note of. They try to ask him about it but Andrew distracts them with a passing co-star. He gravitates towards his fellow actor and starts some sort of casual conversation that can't be heard by the camera you're watching from.

You watch Andrew follow his co-star until the camerawoman sweeps around to focus on the director that's now standing in Andrew's place. You try to follow Andrew, switching from live stream to live stream as he makes his way down the red carpet. Eventually he ducks into a white tent and disappears from view, but not from earshot.

"You still there?" You can hear the smile in his breath as you reply. "Thank you for waiting. And may I ask one more favour? Will you meet me somewhere?"

The End

STAY UNTIL HE'S DONE

You decide to stand your ground. The flow of teens can't last forever, so you just have to wait it out until they're done.

You watch as Andrew's smile and patience grow thin. When presented with things to sign, he places them all down on the table in front of him and speedily scribbles his name on each one. As he hands the items back to their respective owners, he makes a point to tell them to "Have a good night." Some take the hint, thanking Andrew before excitedly scampering away, but others stay. They start asking questions, futile attempts to start conversation considering how many people there are trying to get a word in. They even begin to get snarky when the new pack of teens join, as if upset that they dare try to do exactly what they are doing.

It gets to the point where Andrew stops talking, he just watches as more paper gets piled in front of him. The voices of the teens get louder as they try to talk over one another. It almost sounds like an argument has broken out, but it's just people desperate for Andrew's attention. Attention that he can't split so thin, or that he wants to split at all. You can see the grip on the pen he's holding grow tighter until he drops it.

"You know what?" Andrew's voice quickly calms, though it's clear the ice is thin. "I've had a long day and I would like to eat in peace, so have a good night everyone."

People are definitely taken aback by his words, and even more so when he turns away from them to grab your hand atop the table.

"Sorry, where were we?" Andrew asks you, cementing his decision to the disappointment of the teens. The table of well-fed men, however, chuckles.

"Poor guy. Can't even romance his girl without bein' bothered," says one as he side-eyes a couple teens passing his table.

"The price of fame and good looks, I suppose."

"I must apologize for all this," Andrew says, massaging the back of your hand with his thumb, as if to soothe himself along with you. "It's something I can't really escape from, though it's not usually this bad." He looks from your hands to your face. "I must say, I am very impressed with your patience. It will come in handy later down the line—assuming there's a line to follow."

The End

STILL DON'T GO TO THE PARTY

Even if it's kind of sad, this was part of his offer. He himself wrote that if you weren't interested, then you shouldn't go to the party, and that's what you're doing. He knew the risk he was taking, and what he was getting himself into.

You hold your head high and continue with your night, not letting any guilt drag you down. You're able to enjoy the rest of your night and have a good sleep.

The next morning you see a picture of Andrew sitting on the steps leading up to the party, a rose still in his hand, as guests walk past him on their way home. And that's the last nail in the coffin of your relationship. After that, you go forward with your life, as does he.

The End

SWITCH CARS

With a nervous stone in the pit of your stomach and adrenaline beginning to pump through your veins, you grab his hand. At first his smile is bright, but it soon fades into shock and an inability to processing fast enough.

"Hey, what're you doing?" your friend asks as you rise from your seat.

You give a quick response as you start to lean out the window. Andrew's eyes are blown wide as you place your hand on his windowsill and realization hits.

"Whoa there—"

But you already have your knees on your open window. Just as you began to lean into his limo, having released his hand to steady your self, the limo you're exiting from begins to slip away, turning a corner while Andrew's vehicle continues going straight. There's a moment of time-freezing panic, your heart feels as if it has stopped before it hits the ground running.

Suddenly a pair of arms wrap around your waist and pull you forward. You land hard, with your front hitting something firm. You look to find that Andrew is holding you to his chest and you're both lying stretched across the back seat of his limo, your legs still partly hanging out of the window.

At first there's silence. Your heartbeat begins to even out. And then the man below you bursts into laughter.

"What an adrenaline rush," he says as he tightens his grip on you. He buries his face into your hair in an attempt to muffle the laughter. "Even so, please don't ever do something so dangerous again, my heart nearly stopped."

The End

TAKE HIS HAND AND GO BACK

You place your hand in his, watch his smile stretch from ear to ear, and start running. Like a Disney movie, you and Andrew run down the street hand-in-hand. You hear a couple drivers yell something as you pass but you pay no mind, instead focusing on Andrew. Maybe it's the absurdity of the situation, or the adrenaline was getting to him, but he starts to laugh. He holds on to you and runs all the way back to his home, the two of you bursting in and slamming the door behind you like you're being chased.

In exhaustion, yet still pumping with adrenaline, you both lean against the wall and try catching your breath, his laughter slowly dying down. He rests his head against the wall and runs his fingers through his messy hair. Suppressing a light giggle, he turns to you, smiling like a teenager having the time of his life. His eyes watch you with hazy glee, before they start to drift closed and his lips fall upon yours.

The End

TALK WITH HIM INSTEAD

Too worried about the possibility of being caught in a compromising position, you start up another conversation. For a moment he goes quiet, watching you with a cocked eyebrow before that grin re-appears and he retorts. You end up having to carry the conversation as Andrew goes quiet whenever he has the opportunity so he can focus on watching you instead. His flirting turns into a silent show of appreciation, mainly through the way his eyes trace your body and how he slowly inches closer to you. When you notice the space between you shrinking, Andrew takes your realization as an opportunity to nonchalantly slide his hand onto your knee.

Before you can truly react, however, the car door is pulled open by a muscular man.

"We have arrived, Mr. Smyth," he informs you both.

"Thank you," says Andrew, who steps out first before turning and offering you his hand. "Shall we?"

You accept and he assists you in exiting the car. Andrew slips an arm around your waist and leads you up the driveway to his home.

It's just shy of a rural area, the houses being spread out a good 120 feet from each other. Each has a large lawn—some better taken care of then others. Andrew's home definitely stands out the most as it's of a more modern design compared to the more 1980's-looking buildings around it. The pavement, the paint, the plants—they all look freshly-placed, dating it only a couple years old.

You don't get much time to study it as Andrew is quick to get you two to the front door. After holding it open to let you in first, Andrew slips in and wastes no time in tugging at the back of your clothing. Before he can get anymore cloth away from your skin, the phone rings.

You hear Andrew huff as he lets go of your clothing.

"One moment please, this could be important," he says, a thin smile stretched tightly on his face. He walks around you to get to the phone sitting on a long desk a few feet in from the door. As Andrew takes the call, you gaze around the desk.

It looks to be an old writing desk fit for two people. Despite this, there's not much on it: the aforementioned phone, a notepad and a large cup holding various pens and pencils.

Despite the attempt to distract yourself, you do end up hearing bits and pieces of Andrew's conversation. You can't gather much info from it as Andrew simply agrees and listens to whoever is on the other side. It wasn't until the end of the conversation that some aggression starts to show.

"Could you email me the details so I can look over them later? I have a guest right now … Please, don't start this right now … Well I'm happy for you. I'm hanging up now."

Andrew's moment of stress soon reverts back to his calm demeanour. He places the phone back on its stand and takes a slow breath before turning his attention back to you.

"I'm sorry about that, just a personal project of mine." He walks towards you, a hand extended to grab hold of the edge of your clothing. "Shall we continue?"

It seems Andrew has not given up on the plan he had for you two when driving here. Do you feel the same way? The look in his eyes gives off the same shameless "undressing you" idea as before, this time, however, he seems more intent on going through with it. What thoughts are running through his mind? What is he imagining? Are you ready to find out?

Perhaps that's not your intent though. Must a fun night with a man end in sex? Not to mention, the idea that Andrew has some sort of secret project is enticing and spiking your curiosity. This could be your chance to know him more personally, maybe even create an emotional connection rather than a physical one.

Go With His Plan ➡ **PAGE 105**
Ask To See His Project ➡ **PAGE 20**

TELL HIM YOU WANT TO GO HOME

Andrew's brows furrow in confusion before his eyes seem to darken with disappointment. You don't get to see them for long—he turns away.

"Oh, well that's OK, I guess. I mean if that's what you want," he begins to stumble over his words, and his feet as he stands and quickly tries to slip on his underwear. "I'll, um, call you a cab, OK?"

He doesn't let you answer. He slips out of the room without grabbing any more of his clothing and as he closes the door behind him, you can hear another voice.

"Morning, Drew. Hey, you OK man?" The voice sounds like its from the man that had barged into the room moments before, but with you only having heard one word from him, you can't be sure.

"It's nothing big, I guess. I just …" It gets harder to make out Andrew's words as they drift away.

You rise and prepare to leave, taking a moment to peek into the second door for the room and confirm that it is a bathroom. Open for your use, you suppose—if you want to.

By the time you leave the bedroom, Andrew is nowhere to be seen, but you do spot Zach exiting one of the other rooms, pushing an opal red laundry hamper. The moment he spots you, his concerned eyes shift to a harsh glare.

"The cab is almost here. I'd prefer if you waited for it outside." His tone is not only rude, but condescending, as if he has a personal problem with you and expects you to know what it is and feel bad for it.

Zach doesn't stick around long. He slips into the room you just exited without caring about bumping into you or not.

With nothing really left for you to stick around for, you head for the front door.

As you grab a hold of the doorknob, you take one last look back into the house and see Andrew watching you from the top of the lower-floor staircase. His expression is of a man who is heartbroken to see something happen but knowing he has no power to change it—like someone who has fought for a relationships but is facing the inevitable and just can't fight anymore.

He doesn't wait for you to leave. Instead he retreats back down the stairs as if he can't take your presence any longer.

The End

TELL THE TEENS TO BUZZ OFF

This was supposed to be your night, you aren't going to be shoved aside by these fans.

"Can you buzz off?" you snap, causing the group of girls to jump back. Even the newly-arriving teens look over in concern. Andrew raises a brow at your outburst but says nothing, watching intently for your next action as he hands back the pen he had been holding.

"What's your problem? We just want a couple pictures," one girl exclaims, She's one of few that look angry and ready to fight; the others have a look of concern as they take a couple steps back.

"If it was one or two people—fine—but do you really think anyone wants to be hounded by 15 people at 3:30 in the morning? And when they're on a date no less?!"

The girl's stance wavers, taking a step back into the rest of her friends; they look down in a mix of shame, yet understanding. Some nod to themselves, others begin to leave. Andrew looks on at the scene, a hand rising to cover his lips as they curl upward.

"We—well, why do you get to eat with him, what makes *you* so special?" the girl asks, air leaving her lungs like a toy gun trying desperately to fire like a cannon.

"Because I didn't gather my whole list of friends before the break of dawn just to hound him for autographs and pictures. I talked to him like a normal person, and not while he was busy trying to talk to someone else."

"W—well, fuck you!" the girl screams before turning on her heels and storming out of the building.

Everyone in the restaurant watches her go, most of the other patrons and staff roll their eyes at the teen's display. The group of friends look to each other and accept the situation. Sighing, giving hugs, shrugging shoulders—they all leave you alone and trickle their different ways out of the restaurant, a couple even staying and ordering more food.

"My, my," Andrew says, turning in his chair to face you with an amused smile stretched across his face. "Have you ever considered being a bodyguard? I would love having a strong woman sticking around."

The End

TRY STARTING FOREPLAY

Being so close to Andrew in a space that seems private from the world allows your mind to wander into naughty territory.

With your right hand comfortably trapped between you two, you turn to face him. His gaze turns curious as he watches you, teeth coming out to bite his bottom lip in anticipation as your left hand moves closer to him. A noise nearly escapes his throat when you make contact, placing the tips of your fingers in the open V of his waistcoat so only the thin layer of his undershirt separates you two. You look into his eyes for any objections but find a flicker of disappointment instead. He doesn't give you time to decipher this, however, instead grabs hold of your hand, pushes down flat, and leads it upward towards his neck. He watches his own hand at first, but when he releases you to let you wander wherever you wish, his gaze fixes on you, on your face, on your reaction.

From there, Andrew takes a loose lead. He guides your lips together and never pushes hard for anything else, not even touching you in more intimate places. He is content to kiss you and hold you close, as if cradling you.

As the desire to be touched grows, it continues to be left unsatisfied, making the car ride seem longer than it actually was. It doesn't help that when the vehicle comes to a stop, so do all forms of contact. Andrew separates himself from you and is the first to leave the limo. As you get out of the car and he walks you to the front door, it's clear that he doesn't want to show off what the intent for the night might be to anyone outside of you both.

You enter his home, which starts with a short hall—both vertically and horizontally. To your right is a long wooden desk with a few handy things on it: a phone, a notepad and several different writing utensils. To your left is a closed door, but you don't get a chance to look in, instead Andrew leads you further into the house.

You walk through the short hall and into a humongous room, ceilings reaching up about 30 feet, and floor space about 1500 square feet. The farthest wall from you is almost completely made of glass; the windows look out over acres of farmland. You can easily see the vastness of farmland with how high the house is, though you aren't certain what's growing there.

Back inside the house, there are couches and armchairs in matching shades of opal red, placed in a C-shape around a glass coffee table rimmed with the same shade of red. In fact the whole room seems to have an opal red motif to it—from the furniture, to decorations, to even the walls painted white with swirling patterns of opal-coloured foliage. There's a large chunk of the wall that's pure white, presumably creating a blank space for the projector attached to the ceiling. Under that blank chunk of wall is a fireplace that looks like it might be simply decorative, the same as every knick-knack on top of it. There's only one thing that looks slightly out of place: a small display brick that holds two different coloured coin-shaped objects with three more empty spaces.

Was Andrew a coin collector?

"This way," Andrew says, the gentle smile on his face seeming to tell you that you've been standing just a tad too long, but also that he's kind of flattered by it.

He offers you his elbow, letting you wrap your arm around his before he begins to lead you towards the staircases. There are two: one going down, and the other going up—which is the direction Andrew leads you. The stairs curve in a bracket shape, starting and ending in a position with you facing the same room.

The top isn't a full floor, but an interior balcony. To your left the balcony stretches over the large window that makes up the far wall. There are a few chairs and a quaint table there. On the other side are a handful of doors—you enter the closest one with Andrew.

The room is dimly lit until Andrew turns a knob on the wall so it brightens just enough to where you won't risk getting hurt trying to move around. You can make out some shapes, such as a queen-sized bed, a dresser, a desk and another door in the corner opposite the bed. However, you can't make out any specific details.

You're not too focused in studying the room, anyways, when Andrew places either hand on your hips and his lips on your shoulder. His hands slowly begin to roam, first atop your clothing and then under them.

When he takes a piece of clothing off you, he does the same to himself, leaving you both similarly exposed. Whenever you try to do something, he slows—even stopping his own exploration to give you time to do as you wish.

That's how he acts the rest of the night: slow and tender, letting you experience what you want, how you want. It wasn't a man taking control of a woman, it was Andrew gently tugging the action forward and encouraging you to take control whenever you wished.

Even after the fact, when you lie to rest, Andrew holds you gently, opening up his arms and letting you shift into whatever position you feel comfortable in before draping his limbs back around you.

It's an easy and peaceful sleep that night. And the morning comes to you gently, your body waking of its own volition to find Andrew still asleep. He's not a snorer, as you can tell, and his mouth hangs open ever so slightly, as if his lips are awaiting a kiss. You could do it—take the opportunity presented to you, whether it wakes him up or not.

Or perhaps it would be best if you slip away now; then you can leave without calling attention to yourself.

The sound of the bedroom door clicking open startles you into a more conscious state, your instincts leading you to look over at the man entering the room. You don't get a good look at him, however, as the moment he spots you his eyes blow wide.

"Shit." He backpedals out of the room, retreating hastily and closing the bedroom door quite fast. The consequential slamming noise jerks Andrew awake, his breath hitches as his eyes shoot open and his body tenses. Thankfully, he soon calms, squinting his eyes to look down at you.

"What happened?" he asks. "Are you OK?"

You explain the circumstance that woke him up and he simply sighs, a hand coming up to rub his forehead.

"That was Zach, don't worry about him. He probably came in to try and do laundry."

Well, at least he's not dangerous.

"What time is it?" Andrew asks himself as he looks past you. "10:45? I guess we should be getting up."

He rises into a sitting position, careful not to pull the blanket off of you so you can adjust to the morning air at your own pace.

"Are you hungry?" Andrew asks. He turns only his upper body to face you, a smile so innocent it's almost hard to believe what he had done with you last night. "I could make you something to eat." He sounds hopeful, like he's been waiting for this opportunity.

What a sweet gesture from a man who seems so much more committed to you than the media would have you believe.

Then again, he's an actor. He could have some ulterior motive, especially if you consider how perfect the night seems to have gone. And it is 10:45 in the morning—there's other things in your life you have to get to.

Have Him Cook For You ➲ PAGE 109
Tell Him You Want To Go Home ➲ PAGE 166

TRY TALKING AGAIN

You try again. Perhaps asking questions about him would make things go a little smoother. However, Andrew has no interest in answering any of them. He looks down at you with a sceptical eye, as if trying to mentally uncover a secret plan of yours.

"Why are you doing this?" he blurts out in a pause you'd been expecting him to answer in.

"You made it pretty clear you didn't want to speak before we got into the car, now you're denying the sex you agreed to?" He pauses for a second before speaking again. "Is this a set up? Making it seem like I sexually assaulted you so you can make money in court and the media, or even just to hurt my reputation? You wouldn't be the first woman to try."

He doesn't give you time to answer, probably because he thinks he has it all figured out. "Considering all the questions, though, perhaps you're some sort of spy for the paparazzi, ready to string whatever I say into a scoop." His expression turns cold. "I refuse to fall for that again."

A sliver of previous hurt breaks through his strong expression, but he quickly turns his head to face the front of the limo.

"Stop the car!" he screams to the front, making the vehicle screech to a halt, jerking your bodies forward.

"Get out," he demands, refusing to look at you.

You sit stunned for a long moment, considering your response, but Andrew is uninterested in anything you have to say at this point.

"Security!"

The sound of the front door of the limo opening and slamming shut jolts your body into a reaction. You scurry out of the car, throwing a couple words over your shoulder at Andrew but he makes no indication he is paying attention, or cares.

Your feet land in the middle of a street. Cars drive past you, drivers honking and yelling. A large man stands beside you, his muscles are thicker than your thighs. A security guard of Andrew's presumably by how he demands you run off. You jog over to the sidewalk and you watch the security man close the limo door and return to the front seat.

Then the car drives off, leaving you standing there.

The End

TRY TALKING

Your hand comes down on his, halting his progress. You offer him a smile, but Andrew's brows furrow in confusion. You try to start a conversation, spouting out questions and comments in hopes that he will take the bait, but he looks unamused. He stares at you in such a way that you can't help but feel the shadow of judgement hanging over you. It's so heavy that your voice begins to fail you.

When the limo goes quiet, Andrew attempts to make a move. Despite being held down by yours, he tries to move his hand. However, this time he appears to be much less confident, looking at you as if questioning whether you're going to attempt to stop his progress again.

The battle isn't over yet—your hand is still over his. And you're two humans, why was he making it seem like it was so odd that you wanted to communicate?

Perhaps it's because he came in thinking he was going to get physically intimate, yet the fact that you changed your tune and are now trying to get to know him emotionally was confusing to him. He had offered to take you home for sex, and you'd agreed. Is it not kind of rude to accept someone's offer and then deny it later?

Try Talking Again ➲ PAGE 174
Abandon Attempt To Talk ➲ PAGE 12

TUCK HIM IN

You decide not to ruin the possibility of the sleep he could achieve, so you try to make him more comfortable.

You start with looking for a blanket on the floor you're currently on— thankfully it doesn't take too long of a search. There's a door in the kitchen that leads to a laundry room and a closet stuffed with spare linens. You grab a soft, half-inch thick, royal blue blanket. The fur-like fabric on both sides gives it a texture similar to a baby's teddy bear, but it's large enough to fit a family of three under it.

You take it back into the dining hall and drape it over Andrew, leaving you with the task of moving the book out from under him. You go as slow as possible, lifting his head up just enough so you can pull the book out from under it. Unfortunately, the spine of the cookbook seems determined to bother its author as it grabs hold of some of Andrew's inky black hair. You don't notice this until too late, and Andrew wakes up with a hiss of pain.

His hands come up to put pressure on the pain-filled area. He wakes more fully, realizing his position. Despite a tiny bit of a panic, together you're able to free Andrew's hair, allowing him to sit up straight.

"What's going on?' he asks, fingers lifting to brush against the red indents on his face.

You explain the circumstances and Andrew calms, the wrinkles in his forehead softening.

"You tried to tuck me in? How sweet of you." He offers a smile, and the eyes that look up at you are sleepy yet sincere, like a dog appreciating affection. "You saved me from a painful cramp, thank you."

He pushes away from the table and begins to stand, his legs wobbling slightly as he does so. He holds the blanket you retrieved for him snug around his body, unwilling to let go of the newfound warmth it provides. "I don't have any work today, so would you like to stay a little longer? I can get Zach to make us something warm to drink while we watch TV or movies."

You ask who this "Zach" person is.

"He's a friend of mine that works for me. He lives here and acts as a caretaker of sorts," Andrew explains as he leads you back up into the living room.

After locating Zach and asking for your drinks, Andrew sits you down on the long couch. He retrieves two remotes from a drawer in the left side table before joining you. He presses a few buttons, pointing the remotes up rather than forwards.

An image is projected onto the white rectangle on the opposite wall; flowing red opal designs frame the picture. He hands the remotes to you, leaving you to decide what you two will watch.

Once his hands are free, he stretches out the arm closest to you, holding the blanket out like a wing, but doesn't pull you in quite yet. Instead he waits until you notice the offer and look his way before giving you the same sleepy smile; this time there's a veil of sheepishness over it.

"May I?"

The End

WAKE HIM UP

You decide that waking him up makes the most sense, that way he can find an appropriate place to sleep.

At first you try to be gentle about it, but when he barely responds, you're forced to become rougher. When he does open his eyes, they shoot open and he jerks away from you.

"The hell?" he mumbles as the force of his jerk almost causes his chair to topple. "What's going on?" he asks. His tone is sharp thanks to his frazzled mind.

You quickly explain your situation, to which he sighs in exasperation.

"Thank you, I suppose. I really do need to sleep though." He's barely able to say the last word as a yawn forces his mouth open. He covers it quickly.

"Shall I show you out then?" He doesn't give you much room to offer anything else. He stands from the chair and walks around you, his shaky legs making him waver momentarily like he's intoxicated.

You follow behind him as he silently walks to the front door. By the time you reach it, he has regained some of his polite charm.

"Sorry to ask you to leave, but I don't get very many days off and my body is demanding that I get some proper rest. Let me call you a cab so you don't have to walk, and if you're willing, would you like to write down a way for me to contact you?" He grabs the notepad sitting atop the desk near the front door and slides it towards you. "... When I'm more awake that is."

As he makes the call, you write down your information. After hanging up, Andrew informs you that it will be a 20-minute wait and offers you a seat in the living room. He insists on staying with you until you leave, but doesn't quite stick to the promise. You sit there with him, talking casually, until you feel weight drop on your shoulder. You look down to find Andrew resting his head on you. This time however, his expression is not one of discomforted frustration, but calm comfort.

The End

Completion List

Can you get all the endings?

- ❏ Accept It
- ❏ Agree To Leave
- ❏ Reassure Him
- ❏ Call An Ambulance
- ❏ Call Out To Him
- ❏ Close Window
- ❏ Cook With Him
- ❏ Demand He Talk To You
- ❏ Demand To See Him
- ❏ Do Not Leave Phone Number
- ❏ Don't Call
- ❏ Don't Look For Him
- ❏ Don't Risk Puppy Love
- ❏ Get Back In The Car
- ❏ Get Up And Go Home
- ❏ Give Message To Maid And Leave
- ❏ Go To A Restaurant
- ❏ Go To The Party After Trying To Stand Him Up
- ❏ Go To The Party
- ❏ Go To The Set

- ❏ Hang Up
- ❏ Have Him Cook For You
- ❏ It Was A Gentle Rejection
- ❏ It Was Not A Rejection
- ❏ Leave As Asked
- ❏ Leave Phone Number
- ❏ Leave Right After Sex
- ❏ Leave Without Answering
- ❏ Let Him Be Woken Up
- ❏ Nurse Him At Your Home
- ❏ Politely Decline
- ❏ Risk Puppy Love
- ❏ Say You Want More
- ❏ Shake Hands And Make Plans
- ❏ Shower With Him
- ❏ Slap Him
- ❏ Stay On The Line
- ❏ Stay Until He's Done
- ❏ Still Don't Go To The Party
- ❏ Switch Cars
- ❏ Take His Hand And Go Back
- ❏ Tell Him You Want To Go Home
- ❏ Tell The Teens To Buzz Off
- ❏ Try Talking Again
- ❏ Tuck Him In
- ❏ Wake Him Up

About me, the author, and why this book happened.

Hello there, I'm Vanessa. I'm just a shy girl from Victoria, Canada, with a crazy side that only comes out around close friends, and an insane side that stays hidden. I enjoy food, sleeping and being pet … I am pretty much a dog. A dogfish, possibly, considering I spend hours on end relaxing in the bathtub. I also enjoy video games—which plays a part in how this story came to be, and fantasizing—which plays a much larger role.

Roughly 70% of my daily brainpower is used up by my imagination, daydreaming about both fictional characters, and sometimes myself, in some fantastical scenarios. Ever since I was a child, I have loved to imagine meeting my favourite characters and spending time with them. As I grew up, I accepted that these thoughts were unique to me, but then, while perusing fanfiction, I came across something called "Reader Insert" fiction. From there I learned about "Choose Your Own Adventure" stories and the art of writing in the second person point of view. I was, and still am, fascinated by the idea of breaking down the fourth wall and bringing a reader deeper into the story than simple immersion.

Though it has been hard, I have loved exploring this rarely-used style of artistic writing, and I hope you have too.

If you want to send me your thoughts, you can find me as VanessaP.Writer on Tumblr and Twitter. I will warn you, though, I am a shy, self-conscious person when first meeting people. So, if I reply with something short, it is because I don't want to weird you out with my blathering.

Thank you so much for giving me a chance, and I hope to see you next time.

www.ingramcontent.com/pod-product-compliance
Lightning Source LLC
LaVergne TN
LVHW041636060526
838200LV00040B/1587